序 言

　　觀光局每年舉辦一次導遊人員甄試，由於報名人數相當多（約1500～2000），但錄取率甚低（僅150人，其中英語導遊不及100人），因此競爭相當激烈。在這種情況下，您必須在**成敗的關鍵——聽力**方面，高人一等，才能穩操勝算。「**英語導遊考照速成——聽力口試篇**」的編輯宗旨，就是要協助您在眾多的競爭者中，**脫穎而出！**

　　本書主要分為三部分：

1. **如何取得英語導遊的執照**——提供導遊考照最新情報及準備方針，讓您一開始就有全盤的概念與周全的計畫。

2. **聽力測驗練習8回**——題型、內容完全仿照英語導遊考照試題，臨場感十足，而且絕對不須再做其他的練習。

3. **口試問答80題**——針對英語導遊筆試通過後的現場口試，精心設計一系列的問答，包含台灣觀光勝地、歷史文化等重要的主題，只要熟練這些問答，口試儘管高枕無憂！

　　本書每篇的練習，**製有錄音帶**，讀者應兩者配合練習，以達最佳效果。

編者　謹識

1

如何取得英語導遊的執照

英語導遊考照最新情報
英語導遊考試形式與範圍
英語導遊考照準備方針

英語 導遊考照 最新情報

Good Luck

 1 ▶ 交通部觀光局導遊人員甄試須知

一、報名資格：

經教育部認定之國內外大專以上學校畢業，符合下列規定者：

㈠中華民國國民或華僑年滿二十歲，現在國內連續居住六個月以上並設有戶籍者。

㈡外國僑民年滿二十歲，現在國內取得外僑居留證，並已連續居住三年以上，且其本國法令准許中華民國僑民在該國執行導遊業務者。

二、報名日期、地點：

㈠**北部**：七月廿九日～八月一日，每日上午九時至十一時三十分；下午一時三十分至四時三十分，在台北市松山機場航站大廈二樓本局旅遊服務中心。電話：(02)7121212～462

㈡**中部**：七月廿五日～廿六日，每日上午九時至十一時三十分；下午一時三十分至四時三十分在台中市民權路216號四樓本局旅遊服務中心台中服務處。電話：(04)2270421

㈢**南部**：七月廿二日～廿三日，每日上午九時至十一時三十分；下午一時三十分至四時三十分在高雄市中正四路253號五樓本局旅遊服務中心高雄服務處。電話：(07)2811513

三、報名手續：

㈠正楷填具報名單、甄試記錄卡及准考證各乙份和回郵信封一個。

㈡繳驗大專以上畢業證書正本、國民身份證正本，以及最近三個月內二吋正面脫帽半身照片三張（測驗當日相貌髮型應與照片相同）。

㈢繳納報名費新台幣四○○元，外語筆試費四八○元，筆試入選者，須另繳外語口試費五四○元。

四、甄試日期、地點：

㈠筆試：九月一日（星期日）上午八時卅分至語言訓練測驗中心（台北市辛亥路二段170號），並依試場分配圖所示，至各試場應試，測驗時間自上午九時正開始，逾十分鐘後不准進場。

㈡筆試合格者預定於十月二日舉行口試，確定日期屆時另行通知；錄取後預定於十一月上旬起實施專業訓練三週。報名時請考慮錄取後屆時能否參加訓練（未參加訓練者，取消錄取資格）。

五、甄試項目：

㈠**筆試**：（採電腦閱卷，用電腦卡作答案紙，使用2B黑色鉛筆作答）

　1. 憲法。

　2. 本國歷史、地理。

　3. 導遊常識（含交通、經濟、政治、文化藝術及觀光旅遊常識）。

　4. 外國語文（英、日、法、德、西班牙、韓、印馬，任選一種。）

㈡口試：

　1. 國語。

　2. 外國語（限與筆試所考外國語文相同及所選加考之外國語文）。

六、加考阿拉伯語、泰語、俄語、或義大利語，成績達相當程度者優予錄取。

2 ▶ 導遊考照報考人數

　　最近幾年來，報考觀光導遊的人數增加不少，大約達到 1,500人。其中報考英語導遊的人數約有1,000 人，而錄取的英語導遊不超過 100 人競爭相當激烈。這也顯示觀光事業在台灣正持續成長中，如果好好把握，**前途非常看好**。從另一方面來說，有志參加英語導遊考照的讀者，必須花更多的心力準備各項科目，而且要在眾多的考生當中**顯得突出**，才有錄取的希望。根據這種情勢而言，最好有周密的準備計畫來配合，方可獲得最大的效果。(準備方案參照p.9)。

3 ▶ 考試科目

(1)**筆試**：①憲法

　　　　②本國歷史、地理

　　　　③導遊常識

　　　　④外國語文(英、日、法、德、西班牙、韓、印馬，任選一種)

(2)**口試**：①國語

　　　　②外語 (與上列 4.項所選的語文相同)

　　筆試中的 1. 2. 3.項均採測驗題形式，答案三選一。由於考試目的在於測出考生對各科常識了解的程度與運用的能力，所以少有鑽牛角尖或艱澀的題目。準備的要訣是：**熟記**常識性的題目，**略讀**較深較特別的題目，以及簡單的題目**一定要會**。

4 ▶ 外語測驗形式與計分方法 (詳見p.5)

2 英語 導遊考試 形式與範圍

Good Luck

1 出題形式

英語導遊所考的外語只有英語一科，分爲筆試和口試。其中筆試含聽力與用法兩項。**筆試通過之後**，才可參加口試。以下針對筆試和口試的形式，舉例說明：

(1)**筆試題型**：含聽力測驗與用法測驗。顧名思義，聽力測驗就是考**聽力**，用法測驗就是考**用字、片語、文語法**等。

聽力測驗共50題，每題2分，共100分，答錯1題倒扣1分，50題共分 Part A，Part B，Part C 三部分。

Part A 佔20題，每題由錄音帶播出一個**問句**（question），考生必須在試卷上所列出的(A)(B)(C)3個答句中，選出一個正確的答案，並在答案紙上的方格內，打一個"×"的記號。

例：（*How many books did John take out of the library?*）
(A) It is three.　　　　　(B) He borrowed five.
(C) There are four.

A	B	C
	×	

　　Part B 也佔 20 題，每題由錄音帶播出一個句子，考生必須在試卷上的 3 個句子中，選出與題句意義最相近的一句。這就是**重述**（restatement）的題型。

例：(*The game was called off on account of the weather.*)

　(A) They called their accountant.

　(B) They cancelled the game.

　(C) They asked about the score of the game.

<table>
<tr><td>A</td><td>B</td><td>C</td></tr>
<tr><td>☐</td><td>☒</td><td>☐</td></tr>
</table>

　　Part C 有 10 題，每題由錄音帶播出**一男一女的對話**。男女各說一句或一段話，再由第三者針對對話的內容，提出一個問題。考生必須根據所聽到的對話，在試卷上的 3 個答句中，選出一項最適當的答案。

例：(　*Man: I have an extra ticket to the concert to-night. Would you like to come along?*

　Woman: Thanks. But I already have my own ticket. Perhaps you can sell the other one at the door.

　Third Voice: What does the woman suggest?)

　(A) Getting another ticket at the door.

　(B) Canceling the concert.

　(C) Try selling the ticket.

<table>
<tr><td>A</td><td>B</td><td>C</td></tr>
<tr><td>☐</td><td>☐</td><td>☒</td></tr>
</table>

　　語法測驗有 100 題，每題 1 分，共 100 分。答錯 1 題倒扣 0.5 分。其題型類似一般文法考題，以三選一的方式完成一個句子。

例：I wish I _____ play a musical instrument.

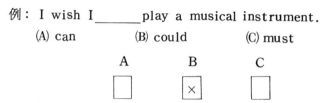

　　在時間的分配方面，聽力測驗約 **30 分鐘**，語法測驗約 **60 分鐘**，中間並不休息。

　　綜合以上說明，可發現英語導遊考試的題型與**托福測驗**有許多相同。不過導遊考試的題型種類較單純，而且答案是三選一，不是四選一。

(2) **口試題型**：筆試通過之後，觀光局會另定日期舉行口試。口試的形式分為三部分：第一部分由考生以一分鐘的時間唸試卷上的 6 個短句，主要是測驗考生的**發音**。第二部分是將 5 個中文句子口譯成英文，以測試**口譯反應力**。第三部分是回答主試者所問的各種問題，有 20 題。前 10 題每題須以 15 秒的時間答完，後 10 題每題有 30 秒的回答時間。以上三部分，考生的聲音皆由錄音機自動錄下，考完後由評分教授**聽錄音帶來評分**。由於口試完全考「說」的項目，所以對一般考生而言，是最困難的一關。

2 ▌▶ 出題範圍

(1) **筆試範圍**：這一項較難定出確定的界限，但大致上可看出範圍。例如聽力測驗可分為**一般日常生活會話**，和**導遊專業場合會話**兩類。

　　一般生活會話時時刻刻都需要用到，當然要會。而導遊專業會話包括：出境入境、在機場、在飛機上、在飯店、在餐廳、在遊覽車上、在火車上、在風景名勝區、在民俗文化區、在百貨公司……等等，都是導遊帶旅行團參觀遊覽時，必須聽得懂、說得出的話。所以對於這些場合用得著的詞句，應有一定程度的熟悉，才有能力介紹或說明。由於這種聽力方面的訓練，一般考生平時較少接觸，因此須花費較多的功夫準備，方可順利過關。

　　至於語法測驗，以文法題居多，主要在測驗考生的**基本文法概念**，及對常用句型的了解與應用能力。所以題目不難，約有高一程度即可輕鬆應付。而且用法測驗方式與一般學生從國中、高中到大專所考的文法沒什麼不同，當然能夠輕鬆過關，因此，大多數的考生都能在此項獲得高分。

⑵ 口試範圍

　　第一部分：唸 6 句英文短句，主要在測發音。

　　第二部分：將 5 句中文口譯成英文，主要在試口譯能力。這兩部分的重點不在句子的內容，所以不會太深太難。但是多多少少還是會出和導遊有關的句子。至於第三部分的問答，必定考一些當導遊需要回答觀光客的問題，以便測出考生**是否有能力擔任導遊的工作**。因此，凡是導遊帶團觀光可能碰到的場合，都在出題範圍之內，儼然成為口試的重心。讀者在準備時，應該對口試的問答特別下功夫，以期順利過關。

3 英語導遊考照準備方針

Good Luck

　　目前國內觀光導遊甄試**每年舉辦一次**，因此有志於此行業的讀者，最好以**一年的時間，長期計畫準備**。萬一決定報考的時間離考試僅三個月或更短，或是平時所能利用的空閒時間有限，此時就必須採**短期速成**的方式來準備了。以下就長期和短期兩種準備方式加以分析，供讀者斟酌選擇。

1 ▶ 長期準備方式

　　原則上以一年爲標準。必須將**單字成語、聽力、文法句型**等三大項準備妥當。由於每個人對各項的準備時間有所不同，因此在這裏我們主要說明準備的原則與重點，至於時間的分配，讀者可視自己吸收的速度，隨時加以調整。

　(1)**單字成語須長期累積**。如果想在短時間內記下一大堆，常會因爲「容易忘」而效果不佳。最好能夠同時注意單字成語的活用，在訓練聽力、做文法題，以及閱讀文章當中把背過的加以印證，必能牢牢記下來。

　(2)**聽力訓練首重環境**。所以儘可能讓自己處在英語的環境中。方法有 1. 把握各種與老外交談的機會。

2. 常常看電視的英語影片或聽收音機講英語的節目。

3. 在不影響工作之下，**不停地播放英語錄音帶**。這一項您不一定要專心聽，主要是習慣英語的環境。

(3) **文法句型應以實用爲原則**，不必鑽牛角尖。但基本的概念及常用的句型務必完全融會貫通，方能活用。

2 ▶ 短期速成方式

依本書內容爲對象，按照下面的指示準備即可。

(1) **第 1 篇**　如何取得英語導遊的執照……〔**1、2、3 章皆須細讀**〕

本篇全是中文說明，不但關係著考試的成敗，而且易讀易懂，僅須花幾分鐘即可看完，又能理出準備的頭緒，何樂而不爲？

(2) **第 2 篇**　掌握決勝負的關鍵——聽力測驗

1. 如何突破聽力障礙……〔**略讀**〕

2. 考聽力須懂得竅門……〔**細讀**〕

3. 實況練習熟能生巧……〔**熟讀**〕

本篇第 1 章略讀即可；但第 2 章務必細讀，才能掌握應考訣竅。第 3 章的**實況練習 8 回**，至少須做二遍以上，越熟越好。

(3) **第 3 篇**　如何準備英語口試……〔**暫略**〕

本篇係筆試錄取之後才測驗的項目，因此可暫時擱在一旁，**等考完筆試再集中火力準備**。

綜合以上短期準備的重點，以練習爲首要。所以聽力 8 回題目，千萬要熟練。

最後，再次提醒想要短期速成的讀者：

一要能捨——花功夫又難得分的項目勿留戀

二要能得——決定成敗的關鍵項目務必把握

2

掌握決勝負的關鍵──聽力測驗

如何突破聽力障礙
考聽力須懂得竅門
實況練習熟能生巧

如何突破聽力障礙

聽力測驗是英語導遊考照得分差距最大的一科，因此常常扮演關鍵的角色，影響成敗甚鉅。

英語聽力測驗真的很難嗎？從客觀的角度來說，我們用最熟悉的國語交談時，都難免會有聽不懂或誤解的時候，更何況是一種外國語言。然而這些聽力上的障礙並不難克服，最主要是懂不懂訣竅。以下列出國人聽力方面常見的困難，讀者只要在平常練習時多加注意，很快就可突破這些障礙。

1 ▶ 訓練聽力須注意的事項

(1) 要能夠辨識連音

一般而言，在英文時，因為是白紙黑字，字字分明，所以，除非是不認識的字，否則看錯的機會是比較小的。但是，若是在聽英文時，情況就大不相同了。說英語的人，常常很順口地**把前後的字連起來唸，成為連音**。這原本是一件很自然的事，甚至，在以英語為母語的人看來，是理所當然；但是，對於不夠熟悉英文的聽者而言，這些**連音卻是造成聽力障礙的最大原因之一**。因此，讀起來很容易的句子，很可能聽別人唸起來卻不知所云。克服這個問題的方法，就是在平時多熟悉一些常發生的連音情況，自己並多加練習這些唸法；那麼，在試場中，自然由於習慣而能夠辨別出連音之所在了。大致上，最常發生連音的狀況在前一個字字尾是子音，而後一個字字首是母音的時候，也就是**子音連母音**；不過，母音連母音，母音連子音，子音連子音的情況也都可能發生。以下舉例說明：

at an old empty house

as I was eating and drinking

not at all

in the evening

They are happy in England.

Do you go to the shop ?

went to the park

a gold watch chain

(2) **注意發輕聲的音和沒發出的音**

在英文中，**語調**（ intonation ）是很重要的一環，因此，每個單字都有重音節，而每個句子也都有重音的部份。正是由於這種輕重抑揚的語調，有一些字，尤其是**冠詞、連接詞、介詞、代名詞**等在句子中重要性較低的詞類，就特別容易被唸成聽不清楚的輕音了。此外，字尾的子音，如 /p/、/b/、/t/、/d/ ……等等，也常常會因輕輕帶過而聽不清楚，甚至聽不見。再者，在字的輕音節或句的輕音部份，發短音的母音，如 /ə/，/ɪ/ 等，也常在唸的時候匆匆帶過，或是省去不唸。舉例而言，factory〔ˈfæktərɪ〕會唸成

〔ˈfæktrɪ〕, enough〔əˈnʌf；ɪˈnʌf〕會唸成〔nʌf〕, you and I 會唸成〔ˈju n ˈaɪ〕。這種例子不勝枚舉,尤其在通俗、口語化的英語(colloquial English)中更是隨時會遇到這種情形。如果對這種情況毫不知曉,或是沒有注意這些沒有發出的音,那麼很可能連平常很熟悉的字都聽不出來呢!

⑶ 勿被同音異義字或同形異義字混淆

英文中,有許多同音異義字。由於發音相同,乍聽之下,有時似乎難以辨認那一個才是正確的字;然而,只要**仔細聽上下文**,則一定可以找到一個意義最切合的字。以下舉一些同音字的例子:

〔et〕	ate 吃	eight 八
〔ˈkaʊnsl̩〕	council 會議	counsel 商議
〔ˈprɪnsəpl̩〕	principal 校長	principle 主義
〔raɪt〕	right 正確的	wright …製造人　　write 寫
〔rɪŋ〕	ring 戒指	wring 扭絞
〔sel〕	sail 航行	sale 售賣
〔tu〕	too 太	two 二
〔wet〕	wait 等待	weight 重量

除了同音異義字外,還有同形異義字,也就是說,**同一個字,有不同的意義**,其發音有些相同,有些不同。在某些情況中,同一個字形的兩個意義是風馬牛不相及的。例如, saw〔sɔ〕當動詞是「**鋸**」,當名詞是「**鋸子**」,但它又是動詞 see 的過去式;wind 唸成〔wɪnd〕是名詞,意為「**風**」,唸成〔waɪnd〕卻是動詞,意為「**蜿蜒**」或「**扭緊**」(發條)」;wind〔waɪnd〕的過去式是 wound〔waʊnd〕,而 wound 又可唸〔wund〕,當動詞意為「**使受傷**」,當名詞則為

「**創傷**」。若是遇到這類單字，最好將其不同的意義都記下來，如此才能應用自如，並且不白白放過認識的字。

(4) **勤背單字、片語**

無論學習何種語言，語彙（ vocabulary ）的累積總是最基礎的工作；無論聽、說、讀、寫，都是字彙的排列。因此，**勤背英文單字、片語是英文進步的一大關鍵**。導遊考照的英文試題聽力測驗部份，內容廣泛，絕不僅限於旅遊專用語彙；所以，平時應多多閱讀英文報章雜誌，不但可增進英文能力，也可吸收新知。此外，對於一些常見的**專有名詞**也要注意，才不會在考場上吃虧。例如，當別人說" **Mr. President** "的時候，我們應該知道這指的是**美國總統**，而不會是其他國家的總統；聽見" **U.N.**"時我們也要知道這是"**United Nations** "（ 聯合國 ）的縮寫。

(5) **多多利用廣播、卡帶等工具**

「**多聽**」是訓練聽力的不二法門。目前的廣播節目中，不乏英語教學課程，而 I.C.R.T.更是二十四小時以英語播音；此外，坊間專為學習英語而製作的卡帶更是數不勝數。因此，**為自己創造一個英語環境**，並不是不可能的事。剛開始聽英文時總免不了有恐懼感，但是只要每天抽出一些時間，持之以恆地去聽，相信不久之後，英文就不再是陌生的語言。一旦習慣了英文，不再懼怕英文，到了考場上，自然可以應付自如。

2 ▶ 聽力測驗中常遇到的困難

(1) **同義字**（ synonyms ）

在聽力測驗中，有時會出現同義字的問題；必須對原句中的各單字完全了解，才能找到正確的答案。

例：My roommate always **prepares** dinner for us.

 (A) My roommate **fixes** our dinner.

 (B) My roommate is a cook.

 (C) My roommate always sets the table before dinner.

 答：(A)

(2) **諧音字**（ **minimal pairs** ）

有時句子中會出現發音極類似的字，如果沒有小心地聽，很可能聽不出差別。

例：I thought her last name was "**Best**," but it was "**Past**."

 (A) She is Mrs. Best.

 (B) She is either Mrs. Best or Mrs. Past.

 (C) She is Mrs. Past.

 答：(C)

(3) **十幾和幾十**（ **teens and tens** ）

" **teens** "是指從十三（ thirteen ）到十九（ nineteen ）的這幾個數字，而 " **tens** "則是指十（ ten ）、二十（ twenty ）到九十（ ninety ）這幾個數字。" Teens and tens "是 " minimal pairs " 當中常常出現的一組，也是很容易聽錯的一個，所以遇到時應格外小心。

例：Take the number **seventeen** bus to the shopping center and transfer to the **ten**.

(A) You should take the 10 bus to the shopping center.

(B) The 70 bus goes to the shopping center.

(C) The 17 bus goes to the shopping center.

答：(C)

【說明】本句之意爲「搭**十七路**巴士到購物中心，再轉**十路**」。從答案看來，原句的後半句是不相干的，故不予考慮。

(4) **計算**（ computations ）

計算題有時也會出現在聽力測驗中，無論是加減乘除都可能會用到。遇到計算題時，必須聽清楚數目字，並細心計算。

例： She has **one** son, **three** daughters, and two cousins. How many children does he have ?

(A) Three.　　(B) Four.　　(C) Five.

答：(B)

例： I thought I had set the alarm clock for **seven** o'clock, but it rang **an hour** early.

(A) The alarm rang at six o'clock.

(B) The alarm rang at eight o'clock.

(C) The alarm rang at five o'clock.

答：(A)

例： 女： How many stamps do I need to send this package airmail ?

男： Airmail postage is **32 cents** for the first ounce and

> **24 cents** for each additional ounce. You have **eleven** ounces here.

問： How much will it cost the woman to mail her package ?

    (A) $ 2.82.   (B) $ 2.72.   (C) $ 2.62.

答： (B)

⑸ 否定（ negatives ）

否定句出現的機會不少，但是有時不容易聽出來。要注意的是，出現一個否定詞，如 **not, never**，或 **hardly, scarcely** 的時候固然是否定句；但是出現雙重否定（ double negation ）之時則變爲肯定。此外，如 **too … to …** 的句型中，雖然沒有否定詞，卻有否定的意義，也需要格外注意。

例： She has **hardly** any friends.

    (A) She does not have many friends.

    (B) It is hard for her to have friends.

    (C) She tries hard to have friends.

  答： (A)

例： None of the tourists is **not** insured.

    (A) Some of the tourists have insurance.

    (B) There is not a student who is insured.

    (C) All of the tourists have insurance.

  答： (C)

⑹ 提及（ references ）

有時敍述中會同時提及**數個人**或**數件事物**。聽的時候，要特別注意每個人或每件事的個別資料，以免答非所問。

例：Tom doesn't know whether his father will allow **his sister** to make a foreign tour.

(A) Tom may make a foreign tour

(B) Tom's sister may make a foreign tour

(C) Tom's father may make a foreign tour

答：(B)

【說明】本句之意為「Tom 不知道他父親會不會准**他妹妹**去國外旅行」。所以，有可能去旅行的是 Tom's sister。

例：Mr. Johnson wants **his nephew** to go into business with him because he doesn't have a son of his own.

(A) Mr. Johnson and his son are going into business together.

(B) Mr. Johnson's son and his nephew are in business together.

(C) Mr. Johnson hopes that he and his nephew will go into business together.

答：(C)

(7) 比較（ comparatives ）

「比較」和「提及」很相像，是提出數個人或數件事，並加以比較的句子。遇到這種句子，必須聽清楚人或事物之間的比較關係。

例：We haven't lived here **as long as** the Smiths have.

(A) We have lived here longer than the Smiths.

(B) The Smiths have not lived here very long.

(C) The Smiths have lived here longer than we have.

答：(C)

⑧ 條件 (conditionals)

引導條件句的附屬連接詞有 **if** （ 如果 ）、**whether** （ 是否 ）、**unless**
（ 除非 ）等 。而 if 除了表示條件之外 ，還用在**假設語氣** (subjunc-
tive)的句子中 ，表示與事實相反的情況 。

例： **Unless** it rains, they will visit the museum tomorrow.

(A) They will not go to the museum if it rains tomorrow.

(B) They will go to the museum tomorrow whether it
rains or not.

(C) If it does not rain tomorrow, they will not visit
the museum.

答：(A)

例： **If** we had arrived on time, we would have gotten good
seats.

(A) We got good seats although we were late.

(B) We did not get good seats because we were late.

(C) We got good seats because we arrived on time.

答：(B)

【說明】 這句是與過去事實相反的假設句 ， if 子句要以過去
完成式來表示 。句意為「 如果我們準時到 ，就會有
好位子坐 」，所以 ，真實的情況是「 我們遲到了 ，
所以沒有好位子坐 」。

(9) 讓步（ concessions ）

「讓步」的意思就是句子有**出乎意料之外的結果**（ unexpected re-sults ）。這種句子中常有對等連接詞 **but**（ 但是 ），從屬連接詞 **although** , **though** , **even though**（ 三者均爲「 雖然 」之意 ），或介系詞 **in spite of** , **despite**（ 兩者均爲「 儘管 」、「 縱然 」、「 不顧 」之意 ）, **contrary to**（ 與…相反 ）等 。句尾也常有 **in-stead**（ 代替 ）, **anyway**（ 無論如何 ）等副詞 。

例 ： I was going to write you a letter, **but** I decided to call you instead.

(A) I wrote you a letter.

(B) I called you.

(C) I went to see you.

答：(B)

例 ： **Contrary to** what Ellen had expected, the city was very nice.

(A) Ellen thought that the city was nice, and it was.

(B) Ellen had not expected the city to be nice.

(C) Ellen didn't think that the city was nice, and it was not.

答：(B)

(10) 原因（ causals ）

Since , **because** , **for** 等字常用來引導表示原因或理由的子句 。

例 ： **Since** he couldn't find the book, he had to pay for it.

(A) He paid for the book because he lost it.

(B) He wanted to buy the book but he couldn't find it.

(C) He bought the book but it disappeared.

答：(A)

⑾ 主動被動（ active and passive voices ）

有些動詞，如 surprise（使驚訝），interest（使感興趣），bore（使厭煩），encourage（鼓勵），annoy（使苦惱）……等等，常常被拿來考主被動互換，值得注意。

例： The painting **interests** the visitors.

(A) All people like this painting.

(B) This painting is very expensive.

(C) The visitors **are interested in** the painting.

答：(C)

⑿ 時序（ chronological events ）

有時，數件事情的發生，有**時間先後的順序**；此時，那件事先，那件事後，很可能就成了問題的關鍵。

例： Would you like to have a cup of coffee **before** we leave ?

(A) I don't believe we have enough time.

(B) Coffee is very easy to like.

(C) Yes, leave the coffee over by the table.

答：(A)

例： We plan to meet at the car a few minutes **after** the shopping center closes.

(A) We intend to drive to the shopping center after it closes.

(B) Before the shopping center closes, we will meet at the car.

(C) The shopping center will close before we meet at the car.

答：(C)

⒀ **直接式會話**（ direct conversations ）

這種會話會提供所有的資料，聽者不需要自己下結論；但是，**記住對話中的細節**對於回答這種問題是有幫助的。

例： 男： Tell me about your trip to New York.

女： It was great！ We saw the Statue of Liberty and the Empire State Building and all of the tourist attractions the first day, then we saw the museums the second day, and spent the rest of the time shopping and seeing shows.

問： What are the man and woman talking about？

(A) The Statue of Liberty and the Empire State Building.

(B) The woman's trip.

(C) The museums in New York.

答：(B)

⒁ **地點會話**（ place conversations ）

這類題目的重點在於會話發生的**場合**。舉例而言，如果聽見對話中有 **books，card catalog**（書目卡）及 **check-out desk**（櫃台）等字眼，那麼表示對話的地點很可能在**圖書館**裏。

例：男：I've forgotten my passbook, but I'd like to make a deposit to my **savings account** if I may.

女：No problem. Just bring this receipt with you the next time you come in, along with your **passbook**, and we will adjust the balance.

問：Where did this conversation most probably take place？

(A) At a library. (B) At a store. (C) At a bank.

答：(C)

【說明】對話中，男士說：「我忘了帶存摺，但是如果可以的話，我想在我的**存款戶頭**中存錢。」女士則回答：「沒問題。只要你下次來的時候把這張收據連同你的**存摺**一起帶來，我們就會幫你改正差額。」因此，對話的場所顯然是銀行。

⒂ **暗示性會話** （ **implied conversations** ）

「暗示性」會話類似於「地點」會話，只是範圍比較廣泛。根據說話者的**用字遣辭**，甚至**語調**（ intonation ），聽者可以判斷說話者的感覺，他們可能會做的事，或對話當時正在進行的活動。

例：男：Could you please book me on the next flight out to Los Angeles？

女：I'm sorry, sir. Continental doesn't fly into Los Angeles. Why don't you try **Delta or Trans World**？

問：What will the man probably do ?

(A) He will probably get a ticket for a flight on Delta or Trans World Airlines.

(B) He will probably cancel his trip to Los Angeles.

(C) He will probably fly to another city instead of Los Angeles.

答：(A)

考聽力須懂得竅門

2

絕大多數的「考試」都免不了形成一種固定的**模式**及**範圍**，因此必可藉歸納和統計的方法，測出一些共同點，當然也能夠演變出一些**專門應付考試的技巧**。聽力測驗也不例外。

如果有二人聽力程度相等，其中一位經過特別指導，懂得一些實力以外的解題技巧，而另外一位則無。兩人同時參加一項測驗，其成績通常以受過特別指導的那一位較高。所以，讀者不妨**在加強實力之餘，略通應考技巧**，免得以些微差距落敗，而感到遺憾與後悔。以下就聽力測驗應考的技巧，提出幾項建議：

1. **保持情緒穩定，精神專注**——聽力測驗不同於一般筆試，它沒有暫時擱下，回頭再想的機會，所以務必時時刻刻凝神傾聽。稍不注意，一縱即逝，更會影響接下來各題的作答情緒。為保持穩定的心情，除了平時應多聽錄音帶做模擬題，熟悉臨場經驗之外，進考場前後可用**深呼吸、放鬆臉部器官、閉目守神**等方法，安定緊張的心情，才有可能獲得高分。

2. **趕在每一題的題目播放之前，先將 3 個答案瀏覽一遍**——這種方法能預知題目可能的方向，而且在題目唸完之時，僅花費較短的時間思考，即可選出正確的答案。同時每答完一題，都有剩餘的時間，先瀏覽下一題的 3 個答案。這是考聽力測驗最重要的技巧。

3. **在試題空白處做簡單的筆記**——這項技巧是要應付含**數字、年代、時間、地點、人名、地名**等之類的題目。尤其是同時出現二個以上的數字或年代⋯⋯等等時，很容易混淆。用簡單的**代號**記下這些項目，有助於迅速判斷出正確的答案。

4. **放棄完全沒有頭緒的題目，趕緊跳讀下一題的答案**——這是不得已的，因為在完全沒有判別根據的情況下，寧可放棄，**決不可輕易下筆**，或留戀不前。能捨得區區一題，才能保住以下的好多題呢！

5. **注意答案紙的號碼順序，不要畫錯格**——這點的重要性，當然不須再解釋。任你實力超強，任你應考竅門把握多麼好，一旦畫錯格，則前功盡棄，確實不可不慎！

以上 5 點，讀者若能好好把握，必可獲得本身實力以上的成績。

本章包括**8回模擬試題**（Test ），後面並附有**解答與註釋**。每回分為 Part I, Part II, Part III 3 部分。Part I 有 20 題，每題由錄音帶播出一個問句，讀者必須在試題上的 3 個答句中，選出最適當的一個答句。Part II 也有 20 題，每題由錄音帶播出一個敍述（ statement ），讀者須從試題上的 3 個敍述中，選出一個與原敍述意義最相近的答案。Part III 則是由錄音帶播出一男一女的對話（ 各說一次 ），然後由第三者針對談話內容提出一個問題，讀者須在試題上的三個選項中，選出一個正確的答案。

每一回 Test 約須**30分鐘**。讀者必須**配合錄音帶練習**，才能達到訓練的效果。

錄音帶所唸的原文，都附在每一回的後面，答案跟在每題原文的右側。而且重要單字片語等還加有註釋。

訓練聽力如果只聽一遍絕對不夠，因此讀者一定要盡量多聽幾遍，聽到每一字每一句都完全聽懂為止。

現在，請將錄音帶準備好，開始接受挑戰！

聽力測驗實況練習 / Test 1

Part I

<u>Directions</u>: In this part of the test, you will hear twenty questions. Each question will be spoken just once. The question will not be written out for you, so you have to listen carefully in order to understand the question. After you hear the question, read the three possible answers and decide which one would be the best answer to the question you've heard. Listen to the following example.

You'll hear:
Is there a scenic drive to Hualien?
You will read:
(A) Sorry, I don't drive.
(B) In my car.
(C) Yes, take a right at the next corner, and go straight.

The best answer to the question "Is there a scenic drive to Hualien?" is (C) "Yes, take a right at the next corner, and go straight." Therefore you should choose answer (C) and mark (C) as shown below:

(A)   (B)   (C)

1. (A) Your name is Dorothy.   (B) Jim told me.
   (C) I'm Tim.

2. (A) Last week.   (B) Next month.
   (C) Four years.

3. (A) Never.   (B) He's nice.
   (C) It's not easy.

4. (A) Twenty-four songs.
   (B) It's a different one.
   (C) I haven't seen him.

5. (A) Number 116.   (B) At the hotel.
   (C) I flew here.

6. (A) No, it's his own.   (B) It's very poor.
   (C) He doesn't like it.

7. (A) Yes, I'm here on business.
   (B) Yes, they're touring the country.
   (C) No, I don't like them.

8. (A) I think it's fine.
   (B) We want to move to another hotel.
   (C) Not too well.

9. (A) No, they weren't home.
   (B) No, I didn't hear you call.
   (C) No, it wasn't hot enough today.

10. (A) Never on Fridays.   (B) Only once.
   (C) Just before I leave for Texas.

11. (A) I don't know.   (B) He's Tom McCarthy.
   (C) I'm Arthur Brady.

12. (A) No, I think I have a fever.
   (B) I don't want to get a cold.
   (C) I slept well last night.

13. (A) Because we want to see a movie.
   (B) I hate fights.
   (C) It's you who argues with me!

14. (A) I love them!   (B) He's a good guy.
   (C) I prefer Chinese food.

15. (A) No, he thinks it's too dangerous.
   (B) No, I'm not going to race his car.
   (C) No, his is a Ford.

16. (A) Yes, I go by Matthew all the time.
   (B) No, my parents call me Binky.
   (C) Yes, it's Reg.

17. (A) He's a carpenter.
   (B) He goes bowling twice a week.
   (C) He has a woodworking shop in his basement.

18. (A) Yes, maybe a little too slowly.
   (B) No, I understand you perfectly.
   (C) No, please slow down.

19. (A) She says it's Sunday today.
    (B) She says it's too hot there.
    (C) She says he'll go there in a few days.

20. (A) Yes, I don't fear flying.
    (B) No, I can't stand the thought of flying.
    (C) No, in fact I love to fly.

Part II

Directions: In this part of the test you will hear twenty statements. Each statement will be spoken just once. After you hear the statement, read the three sentences and decide which one comes closest to the meaning of the statement that you've heard. Listen to the following example.

You·ll hear:
        All three of them have $5.00.
You will read:
        (A) They have $15.00 in all.
        (B) They have $20.00 in all.
        (C) They have $10.00 in all.

Sentence (A) "They have $15.00 in all" means almost the same as the statement you've heard "All three of them have $5.00." Therefore you should choose answer (A).

21. (A) It rained last night.
    (B) We didn't have rain in the afternoon.
    (C) It snowed last night.

22. (A) They cost $14.00 all together.
    (B) They cost $9.00 all together.
    (C) They cost $5.00 all together.

23. (A) Don was still there.   (B) Betty had left.
    (C) Betty was still there.

24. (A) His passport is on the chair.
    (B) Her passport is on the chair.
    (C) His passport is on her passport.

25. (A) Bob is the oldest.   (B) Mary is the oldest.
    (C) John is the youngest.

26. (A) He got up at 8:00.
    (B) He left home at 7:00.
    (C) He got up at 7:00.

27. (A) Julie wrote a letter.　(B) Tom wrote a letter.
    (C) They wrote a letter.

28. (A) The paper is on the pen and the book.
    (B) The pen is on the book.
    (C) The book and the pen are on the paper.

29. (A) He has a blue and white shirt.
    (B) She has a blue shirt.
    (C) He has a blue shirt.

30. (A) Bill and Patty like skiing.
    (B) Bill and Patty like swimming.
    (C) Patty likes skiing.

31. (A) They have $20.00.　(B) Dick has $15.00.
    (C) John has $5.00

32. (A) Jim got a present.　(B) Bill got a present.
    (C) Mary got a present.

33. (A) Bob hit Ed.　(B) Her brother hit Bob.
    (C) Ed hit Bob.

34. (A) Ed is the fastest.　(B) Ed is the slowest.
    (C) Bob is the slowest.

35. (A) She has three keys.　(B) She has two bags.
    (C) She has three bags.

36. (A) He left at 8:30.　(B) He came back at 8:13.
    (C) He left at 8:00.

37. (A) The cat is white.　(B) The box is white.
    (C) Teh box is under the cat.

38. (A) Fred didn't go bowling.　(B) Jack went bowling.
    (C) Fred went bowling.

39. (A) Bob left on Thursday.　(B) Bill left on Friday.
    (C) John left on Thursday.

40. (A) Nancy likes yellow.　(B) Sue likes yellow.
    (C) Nancy likes red.

Part III

Directions: In this part of the test, you will hear ten
short conversations between two speakers. At the end of
each conversation, a third voice will ask a question
about what was said. The question will be spoken just
once. After you hear the conversation and the question
about it, read the three possible answers and decide
which one would be the best answer to the question you've
heard. Listen to the following example:

    You will hear:
        Man: Would you like to own your own business?
        woman: I wouldn't mind a bit.
        3rd voice: What did the woman mean?
    You will read:
        (A) She couldn't make up her mind.
        (B) She doesn't have time for a job.
        (C) She'd like to have a company of her own.

From the conversation, we know that the woman would like
to have her own company. The best answer, then is (C),
"She would like to have a company of her own." Therefore
you should choose answer (C).

41. (A) Red and green.   (B) Green.
    (C) Blue.

42. (A) 8:00   (B) 7:45   (C) 8:15

43. (A) Five dollars.
    (B) Two or three dollars.
    (C) Seven dollars.

44. (A) At 8:35   (B) At 8:05   (C) At 8:20.

45. (A) 514 Fifth Street.   (B) 415 Fourth Street.
    (C) 415 Fifth Street.

46. (A) Black.   (B) With sugar.   (C) With cream.

47. (A) At a restaurant.   (B) In a bus.
    (C) At a store.

48. (A) At 7:45.   (B) At 8:00.   (C) At 7:30.

49. (A) Golf and bowling.　　(B) Swimming.
    (C) Bowling and swimming.

50. (A) She likes Bach better than Beethoven.
    (B) She doesn't like him.
    (C) She likes him better than Bach.

聽力測驗實況練習解答

Test 1

Part I

【原文】　　　　　　　　　　　　　　　　　　【答案】

1. How did you know my name ?　　　　　　　(B)

2. How long have you lived here ?　　　　　　(C)

3. What do you think about Dave ?　　　　　　(B)

4. Didn't Jim buy that record, too ?　　　　(B)

5. Which room are you staying in ?　　　　　(A)

6. Did he rent that car ?　　　　　　　　　　(A)

7. Are they here on vacation ?　　　　　　　　(B)

8. How do they like the hotel ?　　　　　　　(C)

9. Did you go swimming today ?　　　　　　　(C)

10. Have you ever been to Cincinnati ?　　　(B)

11. What did you say your name is ?　　　　　(C)

12. Are you feeling all right today ?　　　　(A)

13. Why do you always want to argue with me ?　(C)

14. Do you like action-packed movies ?　　　(A)

15. Does he like to race cars ?　　　　　　　(A)

16. Do you have a nickname ?　　　　　　　　(C)

17. What line of work is Ray in ?　　　　　　(A)

18. Am I speaking too quickly ?　　　　　　　(B)

19. Why doesn't Anne want to go to Tulsa ?　(B)

20. Are you afraid of getting on an airplane ?　(C)

【註釋】

14. action-packed movies 動作片   15. race cars 賽車

17. line of work 行業；職業

Part Ⅱ

【原文】	【答案】
21. It rained in the afternoon and snowed last night.	(C)
22. This shirt cost $5.00 and those were two for $9.00.	(A)
23. When Fred got there, Betty and Don had left.	(B)
24. The passport on the chair is hers not his.	(B)
25. Mary is older than Bob and John.	(B)
26. My father got up at 7:00 and left home at 8:00.	(C)
27. Julie sent a letter to John and Tom.	(A)
28. There's a book and a pen on the paper.	(C)
29. Jack's shirt is blue and Nancy's white.	(C)
30. Bill likes swimming and Patty likes skiing.	(C)
31. Dick has $5.00 and John has $15.00.	(A)
32. Bill and Mary gave Jim a present.	(A)
33. Her brother saw Ed hit Bob.	(C)
34. Ed eats faster than Mike and Bob.	(A)
35. Sharon has two keys and three bags.	(C)
36. Joe left at 8:00 and came back at 8:30.	(C)
37. There's a black cat under the white box.	(B)
38. Fred went bowling, but Jack and Carol didn't.	(C)

39. Bill and Bob left on Thursday, but John left on
    Friday.　　　　　　　　　　　　　　　　　　　　　　　（A）

40. Sue likes red, but Nancy likes yellow and green.　　（A）

Part Ⅲ

【原文】　　　　　　　　　　　　　　　　　　　　　　　【答案】

41. *Woman*: Your red and green shirt looks nice.
    Man: Thank you, but I like blue best.
    3rd voice: What color does the man like?　　　　（C）

42. *Man*: The concert starts at 8:00.
    Woman: We still have fifteen minutes.
    3rd voice: What time is it?　　　　　　　　　　　（B）

43. *Woman*: This handkerchief costs $7.00.
    Man: I have only two or three dollars.
    3rd voice: How much does the man have?　　　　（B）

44. *Man*: The bus leaves in fifteen minutes.
    Woman: It's only 8:20 now.
    3rd voice: What time does the bus leave?　　　　（A）

45. *Man*: Is this 415 Fifth Street?
    Woman: No, it's 514 Fourth Street.
    3rd voice: What address is the man looking for?　（C）

46. *Man*: Do you want your coffee black or with cream?
    Woman: Only a little sugar, please.
    3rd voice: How does the woman want her coffee?　（B）

47.　*Woman* :　This doll is five dollars.

　　Man :　All right, I'll take it. Will you wrap it for me?

　3rd voice :　Where did this conversation probably take place?　　(C)

48.　*Woman* :　Are you leaving? It's 7:30.

　　Man :　No, I'm going to wait another fifteen minutes.

　3rd voice :　When will the man leave?　　(A)

49.　*Woman* :　I like swimming but not bowling.

　　Man :　Bowling and golf are my favorite sports.

　3rd voice :　Which sport does the woman like?　　(B)

50.　　*Man* :　I really enjoy Bach.

　Woman :　So do I, but Beethoven's music is even more enjoyable.

　3rd voice :　What does the woman think of Beethoven?　　(C)

聽力測驗實況練習   **Test 2**

Part I

Directions: In this part of the test, you will hear twenty questions. Each question will be spoken just once. The question will not be written out for you, so you have to listen carefully in order to understand the question. After you hear the question, read the three possible answers and decide which one would be the best answer to the question you've heard. Listen to the following example.

You'll hear:

Is there a scenic drive to Hualien?

You will read:

(A) Sorry, I don't drive.
(B) In my car.
(C) Yes, take a right at the next corner, and go straight.

The best answer to the question "Is there a scenic drive to Hualien?" is (C) "Yes, take a right at the next corner, and go straight." Therefore you should choose answer (C) and mark (C) as shown below:

(A)   (B)   (C)

☐   ☐   ☒

1. (A) Because this one is fine, and it's cheap.
   (B) Only if you go first.
   (C) Because this hotel's full.

2. (A) At 7:00 A.M.   (B) Around 6:00 P.M.
   (C) Usually at work

3. (A) Right away.   (B) Sometime yesterday.
   (C) Two hours ago.

4. (A) Yes, that's why we talked so long.
   (B) No, the line went dead.
   (C) Every two minutes.

5. (A) No, she has too many books.
   (B) Yes, because she's not fond of reading.
   (C) Yes, so her arms are very strong.

6. (A) Yes, I used your toothbrush.
   (B) Yes, I forgot.
   (C) Yes, there was no toothpaste.

7. (A) No, she's my best friend.
   (B) No, I can't think of it.
   (C) No, it's Mary.

8. (A) About three days ago.
   (B) Only a few weeks.
   (C) We're going to move tomorrow.

9. (A) I don't like Tim.
   (B) I think France is a nicer country.
   (C) I like Francis better.

10. (A) Yes, that's the third one this month.
    (B) Yes, I left it at your house.
    (C) No, I don't know what I did with it.

11. (A) I brought my umbrella with me.
    (B) It's okay, I rode my motorcycle.
    (C) I never go out in the rain.

12. (A) Yes, and he just asked about you.
    (B) Yes, the train leaves in ten minutes.
    (C) Yes, and it leaves in half an hour.

13. (A) Yeah, up on the 21st floor.
    (B) It's just around that building and down the
        steps.
    (C) He lives on Albert Street.

14. (A) It's up on Cadbury Avenue.
    (B) No, it's on the other side of town.
    (C) No, it's right near here.

15. (A) Yes, and in fact it's already too loud.
    (B) No, please turn it off.
    (C) No, turn it down.

16. (A) Yes, it's here in my pocket.
    (B) Yes, I locked it in my room.
    (C) No, I have it with me.

17. (A) Yes, we have to be there by 4:00.
    (B) It's a nice town.
    (C) Steven said he'll meet us in Los Angeles.

18. (A) He asked me to tell you to go back.
    (B) It closed due to heavy rains.
    (C) It'll snow this evening.

19. (A) Highway 45.   (B) County Road 201.
    (C) County Road 16.

20. (A) Sooner than later.   (B) In a couple of days.
    (C) By plane.

Part II

Directions: In this part of the test you will hear twenty
statements. Each statement will be spoken just once.
After you hear the statement, read the three sentences
and decide which one comes closest to the meaning of the
statement that you've heard. Listen to the following
example.

    You'll hear:
       All three of them have $5.00.
    You will read:
       (A) They have $15.00 in all.
       (B) They have $20.00 in all.
       (C) They have $10.00 in all.

Sentence (A) "They have $15.00 in all" means almost the
same as the statement you've heard "All three of them
have $5.00." Therefore you should choose answer (A).

21. (A) Dick sang to John.   (B) John sang to Mary
    (C) Mary sang to John.

22. (A) Mr. Brown has a car.   (B) Tom has a car.
    (C) Nancy doesn't have a car.

23. (A) Jack was on time.   (B) Mary was late.
    (C) Mary was on time.

24. (A) Bill is on the watch.
    (B) The watch is on the books.
    (C) The books are on the watch.

25. (A) He needs one more dollar.
    (B) He needs four more dollars.
    (C) He needs five more dollars.

26. (A) Pam left first.   (B) Pam left at 12:00.
    (C) Bob left first.

27. (A) Ed and Mary didn't go.
    (B) John and Betty didn't go.
    (C) Ed and Betty went.

28. (A) The shirt is green.
    (B) The shirt is green and brown.
    (C) The pants are brown and green.

29. (A) Brett is 12.   (B) Brett is younger.
    (C) Brian is 9.

30. (A) It's still raining.
    (B) It has stopped raining.
    (C) It just started raining.

31. (A) Sue will find Betty.   (B) Bob will find Sue.
    (C) Bob will find Betty.

32. (A) Tom doesn't like Jack.
    (B) Jack doesn't like Bill.
    (C) Bill doesn't like Tom.

33. (A) Sharon has Sue's sweater.
    (B) Sue's sweater is on the table.
    (C) Sue has Sharon's sweater.

34. (A) Eight people came.   (B) Seven people came.
    (C) Twelve people came.

35. (A) Dick was singing.   (B) Joe left.
    (C) Dick left.

36. (A) He was gone seven hours.
    (B) He was gone five hours.
    (C) He was gone three hours.

37. (A) Mary hit Rose.   (B) Rose hit Jack.
    (C) Jack hit Mary.

38. (A) Her bag is blue and red.
    (B) His bag is red and white.
    (C) His bag is white and blue.

39. (A) She stole Karen's purse.
    (B) Joe or Karen stole her purse.
    (C) Joe stole Karen's purse.

40. (A) Jim hit the car.   (B) The baseball hit Jim.
    (C) Jim hit the baseball.

Part III

Directions: In this part of the test, you will hear ten
short conversations between two speakers. At the end of
each conversation, a third voice will ask a question
about what was said. The question will be spoken just
once. After you hear the conversation and the question
about it, read the three possible answers and decide
which one would be the best answer to the question you've
heard. Listen to the following example:

    You will hear:
    Man: Would you like to own your own business?
    woman: I wouldn't mind a bit.
    3rd voice: What did the woman mean?
    You will read:
    (A) She couldn't make up her mind.
    (B) She doesn't have time for a job.
    (C) She'd like to have a company of her own.

From the conversation, we know that the woman would like
to have her own company. The best answer, then is (C),
"She would like to have a company of her own." Therefore
you should choose answer (C).

41. (A) The woman.   (B) Bob.   (C) John.

42. (A) Jack's.   (B) Hers.   (C) Tom's.

43. (A) $4.00.   (B) $5.00.   (C) $1.00.

44. (A) At 9:00.   (B) At 2:00.   (C) At 10:00.

45. (A) Jim.   (B) The woman.   (C) Joe.

46. (A) Sue and Sharon.   (B) Betty.
    (C) Sharon.

47. (A) Ed.   (B) Don.   (C) The man.

48. (A) The man's office's.　　(B) The man's.
　　(C) Karen's.

49. (A) At 12:30.　　(B) At 11:30.　　(C) At 12:00.

50. (A) $13.00.　　(B) $8.00.　　(C) $3.00.

A beautiful view of the Yi Hsien Garden

聽力測驗實況練習解答

Test **2**

Part I

【原文】   【答案】

1. Why don't we try another hotel or something?   (A)

2. What time do you usually eat dinner?   (B)

3. When do you want to leave?   (A)

4. Did Susan hang up on you?   (B)

5. Does she always carry around so many books?   (C)

6. Did you brush your teeth this morning?   (A)

7. Don't you remember her name?   (B)

8. Have you lived here long?   (B)

9. Do you like Francis or Tammy better?   (C)

10. Did you lose your key again?   (A)

11. How do you expect to get home in this rain?   (A)

12. Is there a bus that goes to Tainan from here?   (C)

13. Where is the subway station?   (B)

14. Is Prague Street anywhere around here?   (B)

15. If I turn the volume up, will this music be too loud? (A)

16. Did you leave your room key at the front desk?   (C)

17. Are we going to go to Portland even if it snows?   (A)

18. Is the route to Chicago open?   (B)

19. Did you take Highway 45 or Country Road 21?   (A)

20. How do you intend to get to Miami?   (C)

【註釋】

4. ***hang up on*** 掛斷電話   15. ***turn*** the volume ***up*** 把音量開大
18. route〔rut , raut〕*n.* 路途；路徑

Part II

【原文】	【答案】
21. Dick heard John singing to Mary.	(B)
22. Mr. Brown Doesn't have a car and neither do Tom and Nancy.	(C)
23. Tom knew Mary and Jack were late.	(B)
24. Bill set the books on the watch.	(C)
25. This shirt costs $5.00, but Jim has only $4.00.	(A)
26. Bob left at 12:00 and Pam left 30 minutes later.	(C)
27. Ed and Mary went but John and Betty didn't.	(B)
28. Ed's wearing a green shirt and brown pants.	(A)
29. Brian's 12 years old, but Brett is three years younger.	(B)
30. It started raining this morning and still is.	(A)
31. Sue told Bob to find Betty.	(C)
32. Tom likes Bill, but he doesn't like Jack.	(A)
33. Sue put her sweater on the table and so did Sharon.	(B)
34. There were four men, five women and three children there.	(C)
35. Betty and Dick heard Joe singing when they left.	(C)

36. Sam got up at 8:00, left at 10:00 and came back
 at 3:00.　　　　　　　　　　　　　　　　　　（ B ）

37. Jack saw Rose being hit by Mary.　　　　　　（ A ）

38. Her bag is blue, but his is red and white.　　（ B ）

39. Her purse was stolen by either Joe or Karen.　（ B ）

40. Jim hit the car with the baseball.　　　　　　（ A ）

Part Ⅲ

【原文】　　　　　　　　　　　　　　　　　　　　【答案】

41.　　　*Man*: Does John have your suitcase?
　　　Woman: No, Bob does.
　　　3rd voice: Who has the suitcase?　　　　　　（ B ）

42.　　　*Man*: I like Jack's home town.
　　　Woman: Yes, but Tom's is nicer.
　　　3rd voice: Whose home town does the woman like
　　　　　　　better?　　　　　　　　　　　　　（ A ）

43.　　　*Man*: Can I borrow $5.00, Nancy?
　　　Woman: Sorry, I only have $4.00.
　　　3rd voice: How much does the man want to borrow?　（ B ）

44.　　　*Man*: Does your brother leave at 9:00?
　　　Woman: No, he leaves at 10:00 and comes home
　　　　　　　at 2:00.
　　　3rd voice: When does the woman's brother leave?　（ C ）

45.　　　*Man* : You work harder than Joe.

　　Woman : But Jim works even harder.

　3rd voice : Who works hardest?　　　　　　　　　　(A)

46.　　　*Man* : Will Betty come to the party?

　　Woman : Yes, but Sue and Sharon can't.

　3rd voice : Who will come to the party?　　　　　　(B)

47.　　　*Man* : Ed's taller than Don.

　　Woman : But I'm shorter than Don.

　3rd voice : Who is the tallest?　　　　　　　　　　(A)

48.　　　*Man* : This is my umbrella.

　　Woman : No, it's Karen's. Yours is at the office.

　3rd voice : Whose umbrella is it?　　　　　　　　　(C)

49.　　　*Man* : Will you be here at 12:00?

　　Woman : No, I'll be thirty minutes late.

　3rd voice : When will the woman arrive?　　　　　　(A)

50.　　　*Man* : I have $8.00.

　　Woman : I have only $5.00.

　3rd voice : How much do the woman and the man have

　　　　　　altogether?　　　　　　　　　　　　(A)

聽力測驗實況練習 / Test 3

Part I

<u>Directions</u>: In this part of the test, you will hear twenty questions. Each question will be spoken just once. The question will not be written out for you, so you have to listen carefully in order to understand the question. After you hear the question, read the three possible answers and decide which one would be the best answer to the question you've heard. Listen to the following example.

> You'll hear:
>> Is there a scenic drive to Hualien?
> You will read:
>> (A) Sorry, I don't drive.
>> (B) In my car.
>> (C) Yes, take a right at the next corner, and go straight.

The best answer to the question "Is there a scenic drive to Hualien?" is (C) "Yes, take a right at the next corner, and go straight." Therefore you should choose answer (C) and mark (C) as shown below:

1. (A) You'll need a permit.
   (B) I'm afraid not, mister.
   (C) There's no construction allowed here.

2. (A) No, so we won't go until 8:00 P.M.
   (B) Yes, but the ice might not be ready in time.
   (C) Yes, between the Brewers and the Braves.

3. (A) No, it's raining.
   (B) I love parks.
   (C) There are many children at a park.

4. (A) A hamburger.   (B) A good book.
   (C) Three pigs.

5. (A) At the Grand Hotel.   (B) My home.
   (C) My boss.

6. (A) I like mountains.
 (B) I only want to go home.
 (C) The park is beautiful.

7. (A) Yes, this is our anniversary.
 (B) No, we're not married.
 (C) We've been married twice.

8. (A) 6:30 tomorrow morning.
 (B) Tomorrow.
 (C) Last night.

9. (A) A car is more convenient than a bus.
 (B) Cars cost a lot to operate.
 (C) Buses are so comfortable.

10. (A) There's a good movie on channel 4.
 (B) To the movies.
 (C) The TV's off.

11. (A) For school. (B) To school.
 (C) At school.

12. (A) This morning. (B) I'd love to.
 (C) I'd tell Tom.

13. (A) It's in the washer. (B) He's outside.
 (C) They're in the washer.

14. (A) I saw seven children. (B) I own six children.
 (C) I have six children.

15. (A) You owe $2.75. (B) I owe $11.50.
 (C) I gave you $5.00

16. (A) He is eating. (B) He got sick.
 (C) He's hungry.

17. (A) To Jeff's house for pie.
 (B) At David's Diner.
 (C) Around ten o'clock.

18. (A) Not before eleven o'clock.
 (B) To my house.
 (C) The day before yesterday.

19. (A) Six years in March.
    (B) We're staying with friends.
    (C) Only on weekends.

20. (A) Not tomorrow.   (B) Not anymore.
    (C) Not tonight.

Part II

Directions: In this part of the test you will hear twenty statements. Each statement will be spoken just once. After you hear the statement, read the three sentences and decide which one comes closest to the meaning of the statement that you've heard. Listen to the following example.

> You'll hear:
>   All three of them have $5.00.
> You will read:
>   (A) They have $15.00 in all.
>   (B) They have $20.00 in all.
>   (C) They have $10.00 in all.

Sentence (A) "They have $15.00 in all" means almost the same as the statement you've heard "All three of them have $5.00." Therefore you should choose answer (A).

21. (A) Paul wants pie.   (B) Kate wants cake.
    (C) Joan wants pie.

22. (A) John is more emotional than Diana.
    (B) Bob is more emotional than Diana.
    (C) Diana is more emotional than John.

23. (A) Tom kicked a dog.   (B) Tom kicked a man.
    (C) A man kicked a dog.

24. (A) John came at 11:00   (B) John left at 11:00.
    (C) John came at 2:00.

25. (A) Dick and Jack are the hardest workers.
    (B) Jack and Fred are the hardest workers.
    (C) Dick and Jim are the hardest workers.

26. (A) The coat is on the chair.
    (B) Tom is by the refrigerator.
    (C) The coat is on the refrigerator.

27. (A) Mary heard the song.
    (B) Joe and Ed heard the song.
    (C) Joe sang the song.

28. (A) They want five bottles all together.
    (B) They want two bottles all together.
    (C) They want three bottles all together.

29. (A) His father drank very much.
    (B) His uncle drank very much.
    (C) His father didn't drink.

30. (A) The pen costs $3.00.   (B) The pen costs $7.00.
    (C) The pen costs $5.00.

31. (A) She can come at 6:00.
    (B) She can't come at 7:00.
    (C) She can come at 7:00.

32. (A) Brian killed the snake.
    (B) John killed the snake.
    (C) The snake killed John.

33. (A) Rose was deceived by Ed.
    (B) Everybody is deceived by Rose.
    (C) Ed was deceived by everybody.

34. (A) Diana's mother won't say OK.
    (B) Diana will go.
    (C) Diana will say OK.

35. (A) Jim was tired on Sunday.
    (B) Jim worked on Sunday.
    (C) Jim was not tired on Monday.

36. (A) He likes juice better than beer.
    (B) He likes beer just as much as juice.
    (C) He likes beer better than juice.

37. (A) He won't buy the house. (B) He bought the house.
    (C) He didn't buy the house.

38. (A) Do you have a good view, Jane?
    (B) Can you show me where Jane is?
    (C) Are you watching Jane?

39. (A) He didn't give her the money.
    (B) He didn't understand her.
    (C) He didn't trust her.

40. (A) He thinks about his weight too much.
    (B) He is trying to gain weight.
    (C) He isn't overweight anymore.

Part III

Directions: In this part of the test, you will hear ten short conversations between two speakers. At the end of each conversation, a third voice will ask a question about what was said. The question will be spoken just once. After you hear the conversation and the question about it, read the three possible answers and decide which one would be the best answer to the question you've heard. Listen to the following example:

You will hear:
Man: Would you like to own your own business?
woman: I wouldn't mind a bit.
3rd voice: What did the woman mean?
You will read:
(A) She couldn't make up her mind.
(B) She doesn't have time for a job.
(C) She'd like to have a company of her own.

From the conversation, we know that the woman would like to have her own company. The best answer, then is (C), "She would like to have a company of her own." Therefore you should choose answer (C).

41. (A) $8.00.   (B) $10.00.   (C) $15.00.

42. (A) At 8:00.   (B) At 6:30.   (C) At 6:00.

43. (A) Bill.   (B) The man.   (C) Ed.

44. (A) Karen's.   (B) The woman's. (C) Nobody's.

45. (A) Mr. Smith. (B) The man.   (C) Mr. Black.

46. (A) $10.00.　　(B) $7.00.　　(C) $3.00.

47. (A) The man.　　(B) Alice.　　(C) Mary.

48. (A) The woman.　　(B) Jack.　　(C) John.

49. (A) Tom's.　　(B) The woman's.　　(C) Bob's.

50. (A) He thought "Jaws" was better.
　　(B) He liked it better than "Jaws".
　　(C) He didn't like it.

Test
3

聽力測驗實況練習解答

Part I

【原文】　　　　　　　　　　　　　　　　　　　　**【答案】**

1. We want to bypass the city. Isn't there a freeway that circumvents it? (B)

2. Is there a baseball game tonight at the stadium? (C)

3. Do you want to go to a park this afternoon? (A)

4. What do you want to eat for lunch today? (A)

5. With whom are you dining tonight? (C)

6. Where is it that you want to go? (B)

7. Are you on your honeymoon? (B)

8. What time do you plan to hit the road? (A)

9. Why do you want to rent a car, when a bus is much cheaper? (A)

10. Is there anything on TV tonight? (C)

11. Where did Ellen say she's going? (B)

12. Does anyone want to go to the ballgame? (B)

13. Has anybody seen Walter's pair of blue jeans? (C)

14. Did you say you have six or seven children? (C)

15. How much is our total bill? (A)

16. What happened to Mr. Carp yesterday evening? (B)

17. Where did all of you go after the movie? (A)

18. When do you plan to return home? (A)

19. How long have you and your wife been away from home?　　　　　　　　　　　　　　　　（A）

20. Did you hire a babysitter to take care of your children?　　　　　　　　　　　　　　　　　　（C）

【註釋】

　1. bypass〔'baɪ,pæs〕vt. 在…外側闢一條道路
　　　circumvent〔,sɝkəm'vɛnt〕vt. 阻遏（計畫）實現

　7. *on one's honeymoon* 渡蜜月　　8. *hit the road* 出發；上路

Part Ⅱ

　【原文】　　　　　　　　　　　　　　　　　　【答案】

21. Paul and Kate want pie, but Joan wants cake.　（A）

22. Diana is more emotional than John and Bob.　（C）

23. Tom saw a man kick a dog.　　　　　　　　（C）

24. John got here at 9:00 and stayed for two hours.　（B）

25. Dick and Jim both work harder than Jack or Fred.　（C）

26. Tom left his coat on the chair by the refrigerator.　（A）

27. Mary sang a song to Ed and Joe.　　　　　（B）

28. They have three bottles of beer, but they want two more.　　　　　　　　　　　　　　　　　（A）

29. His father used to drink very much, but his uncle didn't.　　　　　　　　　　　　　　　　　　（A）

30. Jack has $5.00, but this pen is $2.00 more than that.　　　　　　　　　　　　　　　　　　　（B）

31. Mary can't come at 6:00, but she can at 7:00.　（C）

32. Brian was surprised that John killed the snake. (B)

33. Everybody knows Ed deceived Rose. (A)

34. Diana will go whether her mother says OK or not. (B)

35. Working all night on Sunday made Jim tired on Monday. (B)

36. Now that he's in college, he prefers beer to juice. (C)

37. Tom should have bought the new house. (C)

38. Can you see Jane? (A)

39. She responded so quickly that he didn't catch her reply. (B)

40. To think he used to be overweight. (C)

【註釋】

39. catch〔kætʃ〕*vt.* 懂得；了解

40. used to＋V, 表過去的習慣或狀態

Part Ⅲ

【原文】　　　　　　　　　　　　　　　　　　　　【答案】

41. *Woman*: The blue bag is $15.00 and the red one is $10.00.

　　Man: The black one is only $8.00.

　　3rd voice: How much is the red bag? (B)

42. *Man*: Does the play start at 6:00 or 6:15?

　　Woman: It starts at 6:30 and ends at 8:00.

　　3rd voice: When does the play start? (B)

43. **Woman :** I saw John hit Bill.

　　Man : No, John hit Ed.

　3rd voice : Who did John hit?　　　　　　　　　　　（ C ）

44. **Man :** I heard your car was stolen.

　Woman : Mine wasn't, but Karen's was.

　3rd voice : Whose car was stolen?　　　　　　　　　（ A ）

45. **Woman :** I'd like to talk to Mr. Smith.

　　Man : He's not here, but Mr. Black is.

　3rd voice : Who does the woman want to talk to?　（ A ）

46. **Man :** Can you loan me $5.00?

　Woman : I had $10.00, but I just spent $7.00.

　3rd voice : How much money does the woman have?　（ C ）

47. **Woman :** I gave my old fan to Mary.

　　Man : And she gave it to Alice.

　3rd voice : Who has the old fan?　　　　　　　　　（ B ）

48. **Woman :** Jack sent you a present yesterday.

　　Man : I got one from John but not from Jack.

　3rd voice : Who did the man get a present from?　（ C ）

49. **Man :** Your house is bigger than mine.

　Woman : So is Bob's, but Tom's is smaller.

　3rd voice : Whose house is the smallest?　　　　　　（ A ）

50. **Woman :** "Star Wars" was a good movie.

　　Man : But "Jaws" was even better.

　3rd voice : What did the man think of "Star Wars"?　（ D ）

聽力測驗實況練習 / Test 4

Part I

Directions: In this part of the test, you will hear twenty questions. Each question will be spoken just once. The question will not be written out for you, so you have to listen carefully in order to understand the question. After you hear the question, read the three possible answers and decide which one would be the best answer to the question you've heard. Listen to the following example.

You'll hear:
Is there a scenic drive to Hualien?
You will read:
(A) Sorry, I don't drive.
(B) In my car.
(C) Yes, take a right at the next corner, and go straight.

The best answer to the question "Is there a scenic drive to Hualien?" is (C) "Yes, take a right at the next corner, and go straight." Therefore you should choose answer (C) and mark (C) as shown below:

   (A)   (B)   (C)

1. (A) Bill and Peter.
   (B) One's six and the other's nine.
   (C) Twelve o'clock and three o'clock.

2. (A) With Martha.　　(B) Next June.
   (C) Last month.

3. (A) At IBM.　　(B) On computers.
   (C) I'm a mechanic.

4. (A) It was very disappointing.
   (B) Yes, it was a wonderful performance.
   (C) Sorry, I didn't. It was sold out.

5. (A) She will go to China next month.
   (B) He was very upset.
   (C) She cried all night.

6. (A) No, I think it's fun.
   (B) Yes, I play most every week.
   (C) Yes, it's dreadfully dull.

7. (A) Okay, but I don't have a basketball.
   (B) Sure, are you going to pitch?
   (C) Sorry, I don't play pool.

8. (A) Sorry, I'm not used to speaking to foreigners.
   (B) Of course. I love a nice, slow walk.
   (C) If I eat more slowly, I'll be late for work.

9. (A) He never said that.
   (B) That was Auguste Rodin.
   (C) I don't believe that.

10. (A) The lodgepole pine tree.
    (B) Los Angeles.
    (C) Take Route 12 all the way in.

11. (A) Yes, there's one on the corner.
    (B) Right, they take quarters now.
    (C) No, there's a pay phone two blocks away.

12. (A) It snowed in December.
    (B) The town is flooded from yesterday's rain.
    (C) The weatherman said it wouldn't.

13. (A) I dressed up as a frog once.
    (B) Yes, I have. It's very nice.
    (C) I like the monkeys the best.

14. (A) The Empire State Building.
    (B) I like the Golden Gate Bridge a lot.
    (C) I like the port best.

15. (A) Buckingham Palace, in my opinion.
    (B) London Bridge is falling down.
    (C) I never liked Leonard.

16. (A) Only one, to Greece.
    (B) Twice, but both times the pilot turned back.
    (C) I've never taken a taxi.

17. (A) Here's an airsickness bag.
    (B) Every time I fly.
    (C) I don't have any left.

18. (A) In twelve years.   (B) Twelve years ago.
    (C) For twelve years.

19. (A) Yes, it is.   (B) No, I'm not.
    (C) He didn't say.

20. (A) Watch the radio.   (B) Watch the sunrise.
    (C) Watch TV.

Part II

Directions: In this part of the test you will hear twenty
statements. Each statement will be spoken just once.
After you hear the statement, read the three sentences
and decide which one comes closest to the meaning of the
statement that you've heard. Listen to the following
example.

    You'll hear:
      All three of them have $5.00.
    You will read:
      (A) They have $15.00 in all.
      (B) They have $20.00 in all.
      (C) They have $10.00 in all.

Sentence (A) "They have $15.00 in all" means almost the
same as the statement you've heard "All three of them
have $5.00." Therefore you should choose answer (A).

21. (A) Frank is the tallest.   (B) Henry is the tallest.
    (C) Henry is the shortest.

22. (A) Sharon wrote to Vince.   (B) Vince wrote to Rose.
    (C) Rose wrote to Sharon.

23. (A) The dog bit Ted.   (B) The dog got bitten.
    (C) I got bitten.

24. (A) Karen didn't come.
    (B) Everybody wanted Karen to leave.
    (C) Everybody wanted Karen to come.

25. (A) Pam finished first.   (B) Jack helped Dotty.
    (C) Dotty helped Pam.

26. (A) It seems that Paul doesn't like Fred.
    (B) Fred wants to leave.
    (C) It seems that Phil doesn't like Paul.

27. (A) Jill needs some money.
    (B) Jill took the money.
    (C) Somebody else took the money.

28. (A) They have the book.
    (B) Charles gave me the book.
    (C) Susie has the book.

29. (A) Phil is at home.
    (B) It's not raining.
    (C) Phil is not at home.

30. (A) Eric left before dinner.
    (B) Gail left before Eric.
    (C) Eric left first.

31. (A) Betty didn't want any money.
    (B) Betty wanted some money.
    (C) Betty loaned her mother some money.

32. (A) He will come at 10:00.   (B) He can't come.
    (C) He will come at 11:00.

33. (A) Few students liked the song.
    (B) Most students liked the song.
    (C) The teacher liked the song.

34. (A) Sue has red hair.
    (B) Sue has a black ribbon.
    (C) Sue has black hair.

35. (A) Mary was going to talk to Larry.
    (B) Mary was sick.
    (C) Larry was sick.

36. (A) Carol will go.   (B) Carol will not go.
    (C) Carol doesn't want to go.

37. (A) Richard went out.   (B) Mike went out.
    (C) Mike came in.

38. (A) Bob taught the man.   (B) The man taught Joe.
    (C) The man taught Bob.

39. (A) They appeared to be disappointed.
    (B) Tom appeared to be disappointed.
    (C) Tom hasn't arrived.

40. (A) Jim thinks it will rain tomorrow.
    (B) The weatherman thinks yesterday was nice.
    (C) Jim thinks the weatherman is wrong.

Part III

Directions: In this part of the test, you will hear ten
short conversations between two speakers. At the end of
each conversation, a third voice will ask a question
about what was said. The question will be spoken just
once. After you hear the conversation and the question
about it, read the three possible answers and decide
which one would be the best answer to the question you've
heard. Listen to the following example:

    You will hear:
      Man: Would you like to own your own business?
      woman: I wouldn't mind a bit.
      3rd voice: What did the woman mean?
    You will read:
      (A) She couldn't make up her mind.
      (B) She doesn't have time for a job.
      (C) She'd like to have a company of her own.

From the conversation, we know that the woman would like
to have her own company. The best answer, then is (C),
"She would like to have a company of her own." Therefore
you should choose answer (C).

41. (A) $2.00.   (B) $6.00.
    (C) $4.00.

42. (A) Red.   (B) Red and blue.
    (C) Blue.

43. (A) The man.   (B) The man's brother.
    (C) The woman.

44. (A) That Bob is unkind.   (B) That Bob wants money.
    (C) That Bob will help.

45. (A) Fred.   (B) Sharon.
    (C) Ed.

46. (A) 3 times.　　(B) 8 times.
　　(C) 6 times.

47. (A) That she is a librarian.
　　(B) That she owns a bookstore.
　　(C) That she probably has the book.

48. (A) John.　　(B) Bill.
　　(C) Sue.

49. (A) 7:05　　(B) 7:30
　　(C) 7:55

50. (A) That Mary will be late.
　　(B) That Mary doesn't want to come.
　　(C) That Mary will come at 7:00.

聽力測驗實況練習解答

Part I

【原文】	【答案】
1. What are your children's ages?	(B)
2. When were you in Denver?	(C)
3. Where do you work, Bob?	(A)
4. Did you get us tickets to tomorrow's show?	(C)
5. What was her reaction when you told her?	(C)
6. Do you enjoy tennis?	(B)
7. How about a game of eight-ball?	(C)
8. Would you please speak more slowly?	(A)
9. Who was it that said, "I invent nothing. I rediscover."	(B)
10. Which road should I take to get to San Diego?	(C)
11. Is there a phone booth anywhere around here?	(A)
12. Is it going to rain this morning?	(B)
13. Have you ever been to this city's zoo?	(B)
14. What do you like best about Seattle?	(C)
15. What's the most beautiful site in London?	(A)
16. How many cruises have you been on in your life?	(A)
17. Do you ever get airsickness?	(B)
18. How long have you had your driver's license?	(C)
19. Is it a fact that you're an airline pilot?	(A)
20. What do you usually like to do in the evenings?	(C)

【註釋】

  7. eight-ball〔'et,bɔl〕*n.* 撞球中有"8"記號之黑球

    pool〔pul〕*n.* 撞球遊戲   16. cruise〔kruz〕*n.* 巡航

 19. airsickness〔'ɛr,sɪknɪs〕*n.* 暈機病

Part Ⅱ

【原文】	【答案】
21. Ed's taller than Frank, but Henry isn't.	(C)
22. Vince is the one Sharon and Rose wrote to.	(A)
23. I got bitten by Ted's dog.	(C)
24. Everybody was happy after Karen got there.	(C)
25. Because Jack helped her, Dotty finished before Pam.	(B)
26. Whenever Fred comes, Paul and Phil leave.	(A)
27. The money was stolen by somebody other than Jill.	(C)
28. They heard Susie got her book back from Charles.	(C)
29. If it doesn't stop raining, Phil is going to stay home.	(A)
30. Gail left before dinner and Eric right after it.	(B)
31. Betty asked her mother for some money.	(B)
32. Dick can't come at 10:00, but he'll be here at 11:00.	(C)
33. The teacher was surprised that so few students liked her song.	(A)
34. Sue always wears a red ribbon in her black hair.	(C)
35. When Mary talked to Larry, he was feeling sick.	(C)

36. Carol is going to go whether it rains or not.　　　(A)
37. Tom saw Richard come in as Mike and Mary were
    leaving.　　　(B)
38. Joe met a man who said he used to be Bob's teacher.　(C)
39. They seemed disappointed when they heard that Tom
    was there.　　　(A)
40. The weatherman says it will rain tomorrow, but Jim
    doesn't think so.　　　(C)

Part Ⅲ

【原文】　　　　　　　　　　　　　　　　　　•【答案】

41. *Man*:　This book is $2.00 and the blue one is a
    　　　　dollar more.
    Woman:　The red one is twice as much as the blue
    　　　　one.
    3rd voice:　How much is the red book?　　　(B)

42. *Man*:　Isn't your car red?
    Woman:　No, it's blue. And my old one was green.
    3rd voice:　What color is the woman's car?　　(C)

43. *Woman*:　I heard your brother broke his leg.
    Man:　Yes, but he's doing fine.
    3rd voice:　Whose leg is broken?　　　(B)

44. *Man*:　Do you think Bob will help us?
    Woman:　Sure, he's got a heart of gold.
    3rd voice:　What does the woman mean?　　　(C)

45.　　*Man* : What were you doing when Ed got here?

　　Woman : Talking to Sharon and Fred.

　　3rd voice : Who came last?　　　　　　　　　　(C)

46.　*Woman* : I was late three times this month.

　　　Man : I was late twice that often and John was late eight times.

　　3rd voice : How often was the man late?　　　　(C)

47.　　*Man* : I want to borrow the book "Gone with the Wind."

　　Woman : Ask Mary. She has almost everything.

　　3rd voice : What does the woman want the man to think about Mary?　　　　　　　　　(C)

48.　*Woman* : Were these books ordered by John or Sue?

　　　Man : Bill ordered them.

　　3rd voice : Who were the books ordered by?　　(B)

49.　　*Man* : Would you hurry up? The play starts at 7:30.

　　Woman : We still have 25 minutes to get there.

　　3rd voice : What time is it?　　　　　　　　　(A)

50.　*Woman* : I wonder if Mary will really come at 7:00. She said she would.

　　　Man : Don't worry about it. Her word is as good as gold.

　　3rd voice : What does the man mean?　　　　　(C)

【註釋】

　50. *as good as gold* 一諾千金

聽力測驗實況練習 / **Test 5**

Part I

<u>Directions</u>: In this part of the test, you will hear twenty questions. Each question will be spoken just once. The question will not be written out for you, so you have to listen carefully in order to understand the question. After you hear the question, read the three possible answers and decide which one would be the best answer to the question you've heard. Listen to the following example.

You'll hear:
   Is there a scenic drive to Hualien?
You will read:
   (A) Sorry, I don't drive.
   (B) In my car.
   (C) Yes, take a right at the next corner, and
      go straight.

The best answer to the question "Is there a scenic drive to Hualien?" is (C) "Yes, take a right at the next corner, and go straight." Therefore you should choose answer (C) and mark (C) as shown below:

   (A)   (B)   (C)

1. (A) He's there now.
   (B) That's okay, I'll find it myself.
   (C) I went there alone.

2. (A) No, thank you anyway.
   (B) No, I don't. Please take me.
   (C) Yes. please show me.

3. (A) Sorry, I shouldn't do that.
   (B) Yes, I went there after work.
   (C) Yes, I always forget the street names.

4. (A) The door was unlocked.
   (B) The door was locked.
   (C) The window was closed.

5. (A) I just called last night.
   (B) There's someone home.
   (C) My parents aren't asleep yet.

6. (A) They tore it down.　　(B) No. I forgot it.
   (C) It's in Tokyo.

7. (A) It's beautiful. I never want to leave.
   (B) I think they're tasty.
   (C) I don't like the sour ones.

8. (A) Only till yesterday.　　(B) I left last week.
   (C) I never want to leave.

9. (A) I'm in fight number three in ring one.
   (B) I'm going to Amsterdam on flight 1016.
   (C) Yes, I have a ticket.

10. (A) Two-hundred and ten years.
    (B) Usually two or three minutes.
    (C) About four years.

11. (A) St. Louis is closer than New Orleans.
    (B) I know a girl in St. Paul.
    (C) New York is too big.

12. (A) He's ill.　　(B) We're old friends.
    (C) Yes, I've never seen her before.

13. (A) No, of course I will.
    (B) No, not now. I'm too busy.
    (C) I think you're sweet.

14. (A) Name first, number and street second, and then
       city, state and zip code.
    (B) Turn it over.
    (C) Bake it.

15. (A) A galley.　　(B) An alley.
    (C) A gallery.

16. (A) It's a boy.　　(B) It belongs to me.
    (C) Thomas Jefferson.

17. (A) The river flows into them.
    (B) I don't know, I've never been there.
    (C) There are fifteen miniature apples in this bag.

18. (A) Three, he's an only child.
    (B) Over ten thousand.
    (C) One brother.

19. (A) No, it's nice here.　　　(B) No, I'm frightened.
    (C) Yes, please go away.

20. (A) No, thank you I've been to one before.
    (B) No! I'm perfectly sane!
    (C) I like this planet better.

Part II

Directions: In this part of the test you will hear twenty statements. Each statement will be spoken just once. After you hear the statement, read the three sentences and decide which one comes closest to the meaning of the statement that you've heard. Listen to the following example.

> You'll hear:
>   All three of them have $5.00.
> You will read:
>   (A) They have $15.00 in all.
>   (B) They have $20.00 in all.
>   (C) They have $10.00 in all.

Sentence (A) "They have $15.00 in all" means almost the same as the statement you've heard "All three of them have $5.00." Therefore you should choose answer (A).

21. (A) John has not left.
    (B) John did her homework.
    (C) John has left.

22. (A) Tom has a red shirt.
    (B) Tom has a brown shirt.
    (C) Bill has a brown shirt.

23. (A) Dick doesn't want to go to the movies.
    (B) Dick wants to go to the movies.
    (C) Joe wants to go with Dick.

24. (A) My brother is the tallest.
    (B) My brother is the shortest.
    (C) Bob is the shortest.

25. (A) Jane was happy.　　　(B) Jane was angry.
　　(C) Mary was angry.

26. (A) Richard didn't come.　(B) Richard came last.
　　(C) Richard came first.

27. (A) It snowed after midnight.
　　(B) It rained after midnight.
　　(C) It snowed before midnight.

28. (A) We will finish.　　　(B) John will finish.
　　(C) John will not finish.

29. (A) The girl is Ed's friend.
　　(B) The girl knows Jack's sister.
　　(C) The girl doesn't know Ed.

30. (A) He needs $15.00 all together.
　　(B) He needs $55.00 all together.
　　(C) He needs $20.00 all together.

31. (A) Charles will help Joe.
　　(B) Charles must help.
　　(C) Joe will not help.

32. (A) Mary took Karen's shoes.
　　(B) Paul took Mary's shoes.
　　(C) Karen took Paul's shoes.

33. (A) Tom has Gail's book.　(B) Jean has Gail's book.
　　(C) Tom has Jean's book.

34. (A) Chris got a letter from you.
　　(B) Nancy sent the man a letter.
　　(C) Nancy got a letter from the man.

35. (A) Bob was with Pat.　　(B) Larry was with Bob.
　　(C) Jim was with Bob.

36. (A) Meg helped Phil.　　(B) Phil didn't help Meg.
　　(C) Sharon didn't help Phil.

37. (A) We were surprised.　(B) Mr. Stanley was late.
　　(C) We weren't late.

38. (A) Their favorite color is yellow.
　　(B) Their favorite color is red.
　　(C) Their favorite color is green.

39. (A) Ted pointed out where the key was.
    (B) Ted doesn't want to be appointed.
    (C) Ted is usually a punctual person.

40. (A) Mary was late.
    (B) John was late.
    (C) Ed was late.

Part III

Directions: In this part of the test, you will hear ten short conversations between two speakers. At the end of each conversation, a third voice will ask a question about what was said. The question will be spoken just once. After you hear the conversation and the question about it, read the three possible answers and decide which one would be the best answer to the question you've heard. Listen to the following example:

  You will hear:
  Man: Would you like to own your own business?
  woman: I wouldn't mind a bit.
  3rd voice: What did the woman mean?
  You will read:
  (A) She couldn't make up her mind.
  (B) She doesn't have time for a job.
  (C) She'd like to have a company of her own.

From the conversation, we know that the woman would like to have her own company. The best answer, then is (C), "She would like to have a company of her own." Therefore you should choose answer (C).

41. (A) Ten times.   (B) Eight times.
    (C) Four times.

42. (A) At home.   (B) At Bill's home.
    (C) At the office.

43. (A) She doesn't have class. (B) At 8:00.
    (C) At 9:00.

44. (A) That he doesn't like cars.
    (B) That he is a car salesman.
    (C) That he can fix her car.

45. (A) In a doctor's office.   (B) At a drugstore.
    (C) In a hospital.

46. (A) $7.00.   (B) $6.00.
    (C) $4.00.

47. (A) He doesn't want to have lunch with the woman.
    (B) He will be very busy.
    (C) He's having lunch with somebody else.

48. (A) That Joe bought Fred's car.
    (B) That the man is joking.
    (C) That Fred's car is not good.

49. (A) On the shelf.   (B) Throw it away.
    (C) On the floor.

50. (A) Gail and Charles.   (B) The woman's boss.
    (C) John.

Test
5

聽力測驗實況練習解答

Part I

【原文】 　　　　　　　　　　　　　　　　　　　　　　　　 【答案】

1. Would you like me to take you there?　　　　　　（B）

2. Do you know the way?　　　　　　　　　　　　　（B）

3. Did you get lost again?　　　　　　　　　　　　（C）

4. How did you open the door without a key?　　　（A）

5. Don't you think you should call home?　　　　　（A）

6. Do you know the address of our hotel?　　　　　（B）

7. How do you like Brussels so far?　　　　　　　（A）

8. Do you plan to be in Rome long?　　　　　　　（C）

9. Do you know your destination and flight number?　（B）

10. How long have you been married to Betty?　　　（B）

11. Why did you go to St. Louis instead of New Orleans?　（A）

12. Do you two know each other?　　　　　　　　　（B）

13. Would you introduce me to him, please?　　　　（B）

14. How should I write this address?　　　　　　　（A）

15. Is this a museum or a gallery?　　　　　　　　（C）

16. Who is this statue of?　　　　　　　　　　　　（C）

17. How many lakes are there in Minneapolis?　　　（B）

18. How many brothers and sisters does George have?　（C）

19. Do you mind staying here alone?　　　　　　　（A）

20. How would you like to go to the planetarium?　　（A）

【註釋】

7. *so far* 到目前為止

9. destination 〔,dɛstə'neʃən〕 *n.* 目的地

15. museum 〔mju'ziəm〕 *n.* 博物館

    gallery 〔'gælərı〕 *n.* 陳列室　　16. statue 〔'stætʃʊ〕 *n.* 雕像

20. planetarium 〔,plænə'tɛrıəm〕 *n.* 天文館

Part Ⅱ

【原文】	【答案】
21. Mary was doing her homework when John left.	(C)
22. Bill has a red shirt and a blue one, but everybody likes Tom's brown one.	(B)
23. Dick is going to the movies even if Joe goes.	(B)
24. My brother is taller and heavier than either Dan or Bob.	(A)
25. Jane got upset because Mary was at the party.	(B)
26. Richard came at 6:00, Larry at 6:15, and Betty at 6:25.	(C)
27. It rained until midnight and then it snowed until morning.	(A)
28. John will have finished by the time we arrive.	(B)
29. The girl Ed talked to is a friend of Jack's sister's.	(B)
30. My brother has $5.00, but he needs $15.00 more.	(C)
31. Charles has to help whether Joe does or not.	(B)
32. Karen's shoes were taken by Mary, Paul said.	(A)

33. Tom has to get Gail's book from Jean.　（**B**）

34. Chris saw the man that sent Nancy the letter.　（**C**）

35. When Larry and Jim saw Bob, he was with Pat.　（**A**）

36. If Sharon would have helped Phil, Meg would have, too.　（**C**）

37. Mr. Stanley was surprised that we got there early.　（**C**）

38. They like blue less than red but more than green or yellow.　（**B**）

39. It's not like Ted to be late for an appointment, so I don't know what's keeping him.　（**C**）

40. Mary heard John tell Dick that Ed was late yesterday.　（**C**）

【註釋】

25. upset〔ʌp'sɛt〕*v.* 使不安　　30. ***all together*** 總共

36. if 子句中 would have＋過去分詞　表與過去事實相反的假設

39. keep＋某人　使人停留在某種狀態

Part Ⅲ

【原文】　　　　　　　　　　　　　　　　　【答案】

41. *Woman*:　I just saw "The Third Man" for the fourth time. I still really enjoyed it.

　　Man:　That's nothing. I've seen it twice that often and my brother has seen it ten times.

　3rd voice:　How many times has the man seen "The Third Man"?　（**B**）

42. **Man :** Sue, that report on my desk has to be finished today, but I'm sick and can't come to the office.

   Woman : I see the report, Bill. I'll finish it for you.

   3rd voice : Where is Sue now?   (**C**)

43. **Man :** Doesn't your class start at 8:00 every morning?

   Woman : No, on Tuesdays it doesn't start until 9:00 and on Fridays not until 10:00.

   3rd voice : What time does the woman's class start on Wednesday?   (**B**)

44. **Woman :** My car just never runs right.

   Man : Why don't you ask Bill about it? He was a mechanic in the army.

   3rd voice : What does the man want the woman to think about Bill?   (**C**)

45. **Woman :** I'd like to get some pills to make me relax.

   Man : OK, I'll write out a prescription for you and you can take it to a drugstore to be filled.

   3rd voice : Where did this conversation probably take place?   (**A**)

46. **Man :** This pen costs $11.00, but I've only got $7.00.

   Woman : I've got $6.00, so I'll lend you the rest.

   3rd voice : How much will the woman lend the man?   (**C**)

47. *Woman*: Should we have lunch together today? I'll be in downtown.

    Man: I can't. I'm really going to be tied up today.

    3rd voice: What does the man mean? （**B**）

48. *Man*: I heard that Jack bought Fred's old car.

    Woman: That's funny. I heard that Joe did.

    3rd voice: What does the woman think? （**A**）

49. *Woman*: There's no room in the bookcase or on the shelf for this book.

    Man: Just put it on the floor for now. I'll put it away later.

    3rd voice: Where does the man say to put the book. （**C**）

50. *Man*: I'm having dinner with John and the boss tonight.

    Woman: How could you do that? Don't you remember Gail and Charles are coming over?

    3rd voice: Who will the man have dinner with? （**C**）

【註釋】

44. *run right* 處於正常狀態　　*fix the car* 修理車子

45. prescription〔prɪs'krɪpʃən〕*n.* 醫生開的處方

聽力測驗實況練習 / Test 6

Part I

<u>Directions</u>: In this part of the test, you will hear twenty questions. Each question will be spoken just once. The question will not be written out for you, so you have to listen carefully in order to understand the question. After you hear the question, read the three possible answers and decide which one would be the best answer to the question you've heard. Listen to the following example.

You'll hear:
    Is there a scenic drive to Hualien?
You will read:
    (A) Sorry, I don't drive.
    (B) In my car.
    (C) Yes, take a right at the next corner, and
        go straight.
The best answer to the question "Is there a scenic drive to Hualien?" is (C) "Yes, take a right at the next corner, and go straight." Therefore you should choose answer (C) and mark (C) as shown below:
    (A)   (B)   (C)

1. (A) No, but he deserved it.
   (B) No, I don't want to go.
   (C) Thank you, I don't want to.

2. (A) Yes, I will.
   (B) Because her kitten ran away.
   (C) However she wants.

3. (A) He didn't come to work today.
   (B) No, nothing in particular.
   (C) There's no one here.

4. (A) Once in a while.
   (B) Yes, so you don't have any seats.
   (C) No, I thought you made them yourselves.

5. (A) You can check in any time.
   (B) Last night.
   (C) Eleven-thirty.

6. (A) I ate two eggs and a toast.
   (B) I read the paper.
   (C) I didn't make coffee this morning.

7. (A) At Seattle High School.
   (B) On the University of New Hampshire.
   (C) Harvard University.

8. (A) For about three hours.
   (B) I lived here for ten years when I was a child.
   (C) Ten minutes ago.

9. (A) I come five days a week.
   (B) I come in my friend's car and he's a fast driver.
   (C) I'm very lucky. It's just a short walk.

10. (A) Yes, her mother is a nurse.
    (B) No. she is a doctor.
    (C) Yes, she looks exactly like her mother.

11. (A) I'm not certain.
    (B) I'm good at spelling.
    (C) It's a French word.

12. (A) That's a good idea.
    (B) Make it up.
    (C) Anything will do.

13. (A) I'm very much obliged to you.
    (B) Sorry, what did you say?
    (C) Certainly yes. Where to?

14. (A) Where am I now?
    (B) Sorry, I don't understand it either.
    (C) Sorry, I don't understand it too.

15. (A) It's all the same.
    (B) Not particularly.
    (C) No, it was great.

16. (A) No, I don't.
    (B) Sure I can.
    (C) No, I'm doing it.

17. (A) Yes, please.
    (B) Never mind.
    (C) Of course not.

18. (A) Who do you think you are?
    (B) Who else could it be?
    (C) Who's Mr. Porter?

19. (A) Yes, I've seen anything like that before.
    (B) Yes, I've ever seen things like that before.
    (C) Yes, I've seen something like that before.

20. (A) Hello. Is this Mr. Brown?
    (B) Hello. Is Mr. Brown there?
    (C) Hello. Is there a Mrs. Brown?

Part II

Directions: In this part of the test you will hear twenty
statements. Each statement will be spoken just once.
After you hear the statement, read the three sentences
and decide which one comes closest to the meaning of the
statement that you've heard. Listen to the following
example.

> You'll hear:
>   All three of them have $5.00.
> You will read:
>   (A) They have $15.00 in all.
>   (B) They have $20.00 in all.
>   (C) They have $10.00 in all.

Sentence (A) "They have $15.00 in all" means almost the
same as the statement you've heard "All three of them
have $5.00." Therefore you should choose answer (A).

21. (A) John believes that Swiss cheese is no longer
        delicious.
    (B) Swiss cheese is the best cheese in John's opinion.
    (C) There are many better cheeses than Swiss in John's
        eyes.

22. (A) The game is temporarily delayed because of rain.
    (B) There will be no game if it rains.
    (C) There will be a game regardless of the weather.

23. (A) If the professor wasn't late, the class would have started at 1:15.
    (B) If the professor wasn't late, the class would have started at 12:45.
    (C) If the professor wasn't late, the class would have started at 1:45.

24. (A) Mary and her kids go to a nursery and then to work.
    (B) Mary leaves her kids in a nursery before she goes to work.
    (C) Mary's kids go to work before going to a nursery.

25. (A) After reading the material, she was prepared for the class.
    (B) She didn't read the material, so she wasn't prepared for the class.
    (C) Although she didn't read the material, she was prepared for the class.

26. (A) We expected less people in the meeting.
    (B) We expected more people in the meeting.
    (C) We expected enough people in the meeting.

27. (A) The professor said he was sorry that he had not announced the test sooner.
    (B) The professor was sorry that he had forgotten to bring the tests to class.
    (C) The professor was sorry that he hadn't given the test earlier.

28. (A) Mary is not going to return to her job.
    (B) Mary is right to quit her job.
    (C) Mary did very good work, but now she is quitting her job.

29. (A) John will be able to buy groceries.
    (B) John doesn't have enough money to buy groceries.
    (C) John wouldn't buy groceries even if he had enough money.

30. (A) Harry sold no magazines.
    (B) Harry sold only one magazine.
    (C) Harry has never sold as many magazines as he sold today.

31. (A) My father doesn't like fishing on a hot, summer day.
    (B) Although my father likes fishing, he doesn't want to do it on a hot, summer day.
    (C) Fishing is my father's favorite enjoyment on a hot, summer day.

32. (A) Louise writes and speaks Spanish equally well.
    (B) Louise both writes and speaks Spanish, but she writes better.
    (C) Louise doesn't like to write Spanish, but she speaks it.

33. (A) When the production had begun, the actors realized that they should have practiced more.
    (B) Before the production began, the actors reviewed their lines one more time.
    (C) Although the actors had practiced for months, the production was a flop.

34. (A) Ms. Daly gave the class an assignment.
    (B) Ms. Daly gave the students a hand with their assignments.
    (C) Ms. Daly asked the students to turn in their assignments.

35. (A) Peter and Lucy missed the homework assignment, but they turned it in later.
    (B) Peter and Lucy hate each other since their argument.
    (C) Peter and Lucy had an argument, but now they are friends again.

36. (A) Eighty people came to the rally.
    (B) Forty people came to the rally.
    (C) One hundred sixty people came to the rally.

37. (A) We are going to meet Fred and Mary at the movies if we have time.
    (B) We went to the movies with Fred and Mary, but the theater was closed.
    (C) We couldn't meet Fred and Mary at the movies because we didn't have any money.

38. (A) Frank told the contractor to do the work in spite of the cost.
    (B) Frank cannot afford the work on his house.
    (C) Frank repaired his own house.

39. (A) I studied last night because I had to.
    (B) I tried to study last night, but the material was too hard.
    (C) I couldn't study last night because I was very tired.

40. (A) John was supposed to give the awards at the banquet, but he didn't.
    (B) John was given an award, but he refused it.
    (C) John didn't go to the banquet.

Part III

Directions: In this part of the test, you will hear ten short conversations between two speakers. At the end of each conversation, a third voice will ask a question about what was said. The question will be spoken just once. After you hear the conversation and the question about it, read the three possible answers and decide which one would be the best answer to the question you've heard. Listen to the following example:

    You will hear:
        Man: Would you like to own your own business?
        woman: I wouldn't mind a bit.
        3rd voice: What did the woman mean?
    You will read:
        (A) She couldn't make up her mind.
        (B) She doesn't have time for a job.
        (C) She'd like to have a company of her own.

From the conversation, we know that the woman would like to have her own company. The best answer, then is (C), "She would like to have a company of her own." Therefore you should choose answer (C).

41. (A) Too many people are smoking.
    (B) The breeze is so strong.
    (C) The window is bent.

42. (A) She made it herself.
    (B) She had a tailor make it.
    (C) She bought it a long time ago.

43. (A) At his home address.
    (B) At his mountain cabin.
    (C) At his aunt's address.

44. (A) Not everyone from England likes to read all the time.
    (B) People who teach English like things besides books.
    (C) The English like to read a lot and listen to music.

45. (A) That Liz doesn't know them well.
    (B) That he's the one to phone Liz.
    (C) That she will phone Liz if he doesn't.

46. (A) Bring some food to the table.
    (B) Help herself to some food.
    (C) Use the phone on the table

47. (A) The man.   (B) The woman.
    (C) A friend.

48. (A) Go shopping at the new store.
    (B) Find a new repair shop.
    (C) Buy a different car.

49. (A) Join her friend.
    (B) Stay inside.
    (C) Sketch the tree.

50. (A) He was very brave.
    (B) He's a guide in the forest.
    (C) He heated the metal.

聽力測驗實況練習解答

Part I

【原文】	【答案】
1. Did you enjoy hitting him?	（A）
2. Why is she crying?	（B）
3. Did anything unusual happen at work today?	（B）
4. Didn't you make reservations for us?	（C）
5. When is check-out time?	（C）
6. What did you eat for breakfast?	（A）
7. Where did your son attend university?	（C）
8. Did you grow up in this neighborhood?	（B）
9. How long does it take you to come to school?	（C）
10. Is she a nurse like her mother?	（B）
11. How do you spell that word?	（A）
12.（Handing a menu to B）What will you have?	（C）
13. Would you mind giving me a ride to Grand Central Station?	（B）
14. Could you give me some help with this problem?	（B）
15. Did you like the film?	（B）
16. Can you help me for a moment?	（B）
17. Do you mind opening the window?	（C）
18. Is that you, Uncle Arthur?	（B）
19. Haven't you ever seen anything like that before?	（C）

20. Hello. Is this Mrs. Brown speaking? （C）

【註釋】

5. *check out* 付款；結帳

Part Ⅱ

【原文】 　　　　　　　　　　　　　　　　　　　　　　　　【答案】

21. According to John, there's no better cheese than Swiss
    cheese. （B）

22. The game will be held, rain or shine. （C）

23. The class should have begun at 1:15, but the professor
    was half an hour late. （A）

24. Mary takes her children to a nursery on her way to
    work. （B）

25. Had she read the material, she would have been pre-
    pared for class. （B）

26. Fewer people came to the meeting than we had
    expected. （B）

27. The professor apologized for not announcing the test
    earlier. （A）

28. Mary is leaving her job for good. （A）

29. John has some money, but not enough to buy groceries. （B）

30. Harry spent five hours knocking on doors, but he didn't
    sell a single magazine. （A）

31. My father likes nothing better than fishing on a hot,
    summer day. （C）

32. Louise writes Spanish as well as she speaks it. （**A**）

33. The actors went over their lines once more before the
production began. （**B**）

34. Ms. Daly asked the students to hand in their assign-
ments. （**C**）

35. Peter and Lucy had a quarrel, but they soon made up. （**C**）

36. They expected eighty people at the rally, but twice
that many showed up. （**C**）

37. We were supposed to meet Fred and Mary at the movies,
but we're broke. （**C**）

38. The contractor said the repairs on Frank's house would
be very expensive, but Frank decided to have the work
done. （**A**）

39. I should have studied last night, but I was too tired. （**C**）

40. John refused to go to the banquet although he was going
to receive an award. （**C**）

【註釋】

22. *rain or shine* 不論晴雨

25. Had she read the material = *If* she had read the material
→與過去事實相反的假設　　28. *for good* 永遠（＝forever）

31. *like nothing better than* ～ 最喜歡～

33. lines〔laɪnz〕*n.* 臺詞　*go over* 複習

35. *make up* 言歸於好

37. broke〔brok〕*adj.* 沒有錢的；破產的

38. contractor〔kənˈtræntɚ；ˈkɑntræktɚ〕*n.* 承造廠；包商

39. 「should ＋完成式」表過去該做 而未做。

Part Ⅲ

【原文】   【答案】

41. *Woman*: This room is so stuffy, I can hardly breathe.

   Man: I think they should ban smoking here, don't you?

   3rd voice: Why is the woman complaining?   （**A**）

42. *Man*: Did you make your suit? It's very elegant.

   Woman: I couldn't have done all this tailoring, I had it made.

   3rd voice: How did the woman get her suit?   （**B**）

43. *Woman*: Do you have an address where I can write to you?

   Man: No, I'll be hiking in the mountains most of the time. But if you write to me at my aunt's house, she'll hold my mail until I get there.

   3rd voice: Where should the woman write to her friend? （**C**）

44. *Woman*: Professor Williams helped me so much that I'm thinking of buying him a book of poetry.

   Man: I think you'd get him a record. Just because he's an English teacher doesn't mean that all he does is read.

   3rd voice: What does the man mean?   （**B**）

45. *Man*: How about phoning Liz and asking her to join us for dinner?

   Woman: I think you should phone her. She hardly knows who I am.

   3rd voice: What does the woman mean?   （**B**）

46.　*Woman*: Excuse me, would you mind if I use your phone?

　　　Man: Help yourself. It's on the table over there.

　3rd voice: What did the man tell the woman to do?　　（ C ）

47.　　*Man*: Did you have your friend type your term paper?

　Woman: I did it myself.

　3rd voice: Who typed the paper?　　　　　　　　（ B ）

48.　　*Man*: My car is in the repair shop again.

　Woman: Maybe you shoule consider trading it in for a new one.

　3rd voice: What does the woman think the man should do?　　（ C ）

49.　　*Man*: It's such a nice warm day. I think I'll go write my report under a tree.

　Woman: I'd like to join you, but I find it hard to work outside.

　3rd voice: What is the woman going to do?　　　（ B ）

50.　　*Man*: Peter was given a medal for helping put out a forest fire.

　Woman: He certainly showed a lot of courage.

　3rd voice: What did the woman say about Peter?　　（ A ）

聽力測驗實況練習 / Test 7

Part I

Directions: In this part of the test, you will hear twenty questions. Each question will be spoken just once. The question will not be written out for you, so you have to listen carefully in order to understand the question. After you hear the question, read the three possible answers and decide which one would be the best answer to the question you've heard. Listen to the following example.
　　　You'll hear:
　　　　Is there a scenic drive to Hualien?
　　　You will read:
　　　　(A) Sorry, I don't drive.
　　　　(B) In my car.
　　　　(C) Yes, take a right at the next corner, and
　　　　　　go straight.
The best answer to the question "Is there a scenic drive to Hualien?" is (C) "Yes, take a right at the next corner, and go straight." Therefore you should choose answer (C) and mark (C) as shown below:
　　　(A)　　　　　　(B)　　　　　　(C)

　　　□　　　　　　□　　　　　　☒

1. (A) No, thank you. I can manage.
　 (B) Don't know him.
　 (C) Yes, I'm okay. Thanks.

2. (A) I don't feel like seeing your brother.
　 (B) Her mother died two years ago.
　 (C) Yes. She's coming next Friday.

3. (A) Leave me alone.
　 (B) Why should you?
　 (C) I would be pleased to.

4. (A) The bank's right over there.
　 (B) Sure. Take a right at the next corner.
　 (C) Sure. In my kitchen.

5. (A) This spring for sure.
   (B) Just recently.
   (C) With my classmates.

6. (A) It's Jim.
   (B) I wasn't in school yesterday, either.
   (C) Today's a school holiday.

7. (A) Yes, it was great.
   (B) No, it was terrible.
   (C) Yes, it was the worst day of the year.

8. (A) No way. This is already the lowest price in town.
   (B) No way. You charge too much.
   (C) No way. You're a poor man.

9. (A) No, usually only once a week.
   (B) Sometimes on Sundays.
   (C) No, almost every day.

10. (A) Twenty-four hours a day.
    (B) No, I don't let them watch much.
    (C) We watch programs together.

11. (A) Okay,but I'll need it back by tomorrow.
    (B) No, I'll need in before a week is up.
    (C) No, I'll pick it up next week, then.

12. (A) She has a daughter.
    (B) No, divorced.
    (C) Her father died at a young age.

13. (A) She was being polite.
    (B) He didn't want to seem pushy.
    (C) She hates races.

14. (A) Yes, I do.
    (B) No, I don't.
    (C) No, I wouldn't.

15. (A) There are six rooms in my house.
    (B) There are seven of us.
    (C) Who's Ned?

16. (A) I just called my daughter.
    (B) By all means.
    (C) I went to Las Vegas for several weeks.

17. (A) Yes, there is.
    (B) Yes, I am.
    (C) I don't see it.

18. (A) Yes, she did.
    (B) I don't remember him.
    (C) No, she stayed home in bed.

19. (A) I think it's nice.
    (B) I think he's nice.
    (C) No, thank you.

20. (A) On Saturady.
    (B) He's next to mine.
    (C) It's next to mine.

Part II

<u>Directions</u>: In this part of the test you will hear twenty
statements. Each statement will be spoken just once.
After you hear the statement, read the three sentences
and decide which one comes closest to the meaning of the
statement that you've heard. Listen to the following
example.

> You'll hear:
>   All three of them have $5.00.
> You will read:
>   (A) They have $15.00 in all.
>   (B) They have $20.00 in all.
>   (C) They have $10.00 in all.

Sentence (A) "They have $15.00 in all" means almost the
same as the statement you've heard "All three of them
have $5.00." Therefore you should choose answer (A).

21. (A) Carol didn't want to go.
    (B) Frank wanted Carol to go.
    (C) Frank wanted to go.

22. (A) Dick came home at 10:30.
    (B) Tom came home at 9:00.
    (C) Larry came home at 10:30.

23. (A) They liked his new songs.
    (B) They didn't like his old songs.
    (C) They liked his old songs.

24. (A) His sister played the piano.
    (B) His sister did Bob's homework.
    (C) Bob did his homework.

25. (A) They haven't called.
    (B) They aren't coming.
    (C) They have called.

26. (A) Betty has a blue sweater.
    (B) Sue has a blue sweater.
    (C) Mary has a black sweater.

27. (A) The total is $53.00.
    (B) The total is $18.00.
    (C) The total is $52.00.

28. (A) John drove to Chicago.
    (B) Ed drove to Chicago.
    (C) John drove from Chicago to Detroit.

29. (A) He sent a package to his father and mother.
    (B) He sent a package to his father.
    (C) He sent a letter to his father.

30. (A) Robert is at school.
    (B) Ted is at school.
    (C) Jack isn't at school.

31. (A) Charles is the worst student.
    (B) Ed is the worst student.
    (C) Ed is the best student.

32. (A) Pam has her cat.
    (B) Somebody took Pam's cat.
    (C) Chuck took Gail's cat.

33. (A) He has $10.00.   (B) He has $40.00.
    (C) He has $50.00.

34. (A) My sister is here.   (B) Bob is here.
    (C) My sister did not come.

35. (A) Rose called Henry.   (B) Henry called Mike.
    (C) Mike called Rose.

36. (A) Sue hit John.   (B) Bill hit John.
    (C) John hit Bill.

37. (A) The movie starts at 8:30.
    (B) Jack works until 8:00.
    (C) The movie starts at 8:00.

38. (A) Jim doesn't want to go.
    (B) My father wants me to go.
    (C) Jim wants to go.

39. (A) There are two books on the chair.
    (B) There is one book on the floor.
    (C) There are four books all together.

40. (A) The doctor called her up long ago.
    (B) Dr. Calder proceeded with the project.
    (C) Dr. Calder decided to give up the project.

Part III

Directions: In this part of the test, you will hear ten
short conversations between two speakers. At the end of
each conversation, a third voice will ask a question
about what was said. The question will be spoken just
once. After you hear the conversation and the question
about it, read the three possible answers and decide
which one would be the best answer to the question you've
heard. Listen to the following example:

> You will hear:
>   Man: Would you like to own your own business?
>   woman: I wouldn't mind a bit.
>   3rd voice: What did the woman mean?
> You will read:
>   (A) She couldn't make up her mind.
>   (B) She doesn't have time for a job.
>   (C) She'd like to have a company of her own.

From the conversation, we know that the woman would like
to have her own company. The best answer, then is (C),
"She would like to have a company of her own." Therefore
you should choose answer (C).

41. (A) Dr. Pepper.   (B) The nurse.
    (C) Dr. Brown.

42. (A) Mary.   (B) Mary and Rose.
    (C) Rose.

43. (A) At a typewriter repair shop.
    (B) On the street.
    (C) In an office.

44. (A) The one for $3:00.
    (B) Neither.
    (C) The one for $4.95.

45. (A) That Mr. Smith is very kind.
    (B) That the man should not worry.
    (C) That she is worried.

46. (A) Eight.   (B) Two.
    (C) Six.

47. (A) She doesn't like it.
    (B) She prefers it to his other works.
    (C) She likes it.

48. (A) Type some letters.
    (B) Help the man.
    (C) Go home.

49. (A) He likes his boss.
    (B) He will have to work late.
    (C) He won't work late.

50. (A) He's good at home.
    (B) He's good at school.
    (C) The man doesn't like him.

Test
7

聽力測驗實況練習解答

Part I

【原文】　　　　　　　　　　　　　　　　　　　　　　　【答案】

1. Can I help you carry your bags? （A）

2. Is your mother coming to visit? （C）

3. Will you come to my office at three tomorrow, please? （C）

4. Would you please direct me to the post office? （B）

5. When are you going to graduate? （A）

6. Why aren't you in school today? （C）

7. Was yesterday a bad day for you? （C）

8. Can I get three for the price of two? （A）

9. Does she work overtime quite often? （A）

10. Do your children always watch TV? （B）

11. Can you leave this with me for a week? （B）

12. Is she married? （B）

13. Why didn't she say she wanted to go see the races? （A）

14. Would you happen to know the Mitchells? （C）

15. How big is your family, Ned? （B）

16. What did you do over summer vacation, Mrs. White? （C）

17. Are you going to the big match on Saturday, Jim? （B）

18. Didn't she attend classes yesterday? （C）

19. What do you think of my new tape deck? （A）

20. Where is Alfred's house? （C）

【註釋】

8. get three for the price of two 付兩份的錢買三份東西

Part Ⅱ

【原文】　　　　　　　　　　　　　　　　　【答案】

21. Carol expected to go and so did Frank. 　　　(C)

22. Larry came home at 9:00, but Dick and Tom didn't
　　arrive until 10:30.　　　　　　　　　　　(A)

23. The singer was surprised that they liked his old songs
　　but not his new ones.　　　　　　　　　　(C)

24. While Bob played the piano his sister did his homework
　　for him.　　　　　　　　　　　　　　　(B)

25. They should have called by now if they aren't coming.　(A)

26. Sue's red and blue sweater is as nice as Mary's black
　　one or Betty's orange one.　　　　　　　　(C)

27. The books are $15.00, the pen $1.00, and the notebooks
　　$2.00.　　　　　　　　　　　　　　　　(C)

28. John drove to Chicago and then Ed drove to Detroit.　(A)

29. John sent a package to his father and a letter to his
　　mother.　　　　　　　　　　　　　　　(B)

30. Unless Robert goes to school, he won't see Ted or
　　Jack today.　　　　　　　　　　　　　　(B)

31. Charles is a better student than Paul but not than
　　Ed.　　　　　　　　　　　　　　　　　(C)

32. Pam's cat was taken by Chuck or Gail.　　　(B)

33. If my brother gets ten more dollars, he'll have fifty. （ B ）

34. When my sister first got here, Bob was still here. （ A ）

35. Mary had to wait for Mike to call Rose and Henry. （ C ）

36. Sue was told John got hit by Bill. （ B ）

37. The movie starts at 8:00, but Phil works until 8:30
    and Jack until 9:00. （ C ）

38. Jim wanted to go, but his father said he shouldn't. （ C ）

39. There's a book on the table, another on the chair, and
    two on the floor. （ C ）

40. Doctor Calder had worked on the project too long to
    give up. （ B ）

【註釋】

25. 「should＋完成式」表過去該做而未做   27. $15+1+2=18$

33. $50-10=40$ 39. $1+1+2=4$ 40. too … to ～ 太…而不能～

Part Ⅲ

【原文】   【答案】

41.   *Man*: Nurse, I'd like to see Dr. Brown.

    Woman: I'm sorry, but he isn't in today. Dr. Johnson
             or Dr. Pepper will be able to see you, though.

    3rd voice: Who does the man want to see? （ C ）

42.   *Woman*: Isn't Rose coming to the party?

    Man: Mary is coming, but Rose and Sue both have
           to work.

    3rd voice: Who is coming to the party? （ A ）

43.   *Man*: Joan, this typewriter doesn't seem to be working right.

   Woman: Why don't you ask Betty to look at it? She knows everything about typewriters.

   3rd voice: Where did this conversation probably take place? (**C**)

44. *Woman*: This copy of Roots costs $4.95, but that one is only $3.00. Why is it less expensive?

   Man: The one for $3.00 was printed in England.

   3rd voice: Which copy was most probably printed in the United States?   (**C**)

45.   *Man*: Mr. Smith just said that if I am late again, he will fire me.

   Woman: Don't let it get you down. He always talks like that.

   3rd voice: What does the woman mean?   (**B**)

46. *Woman*: I've had four colds this winter and I think I'm catching another one.

   Man: I've only had half that many, but my wife has had six.

   3rd voice: How many colds has the man had?   (**B**)

47.   *Man*: I really enjoy listening to Beethoven's Fifth Symphony.

   Woman: It is very nice, but I much prefer some of his other works.

   3rd voice: What does the woman think of Beethoven's Fifth Symphony?   (**C**)

48.   *Man* : If you give me a hand, I can get this work
       done in about thirty minutes.

  Woman : I would, but Mr. Miller told me to type these
       letters before I go home.

 3rd voice : What is the woman going to do?   (A)

49. *Woman* : Do you think your boss will expect you to work
       late again tonight?

   Man : Does the sun come up in the east?

 3rd voice : What does the man mean?   (B)

50. *Woman* : Johnnie is really a naughty little boy.

   Man : He's not so bad really. At home he's actually
       quite good.

 3rd voice : What does the man want the woman to
       think about Johnnie?   (A)

聽力測驗實況練習 / Test 8

Part I

Directions: In this part of the test, you will hear twenty questions. Each question will be spoken just once. The question will not be written out for you, so you have to listen carefully in order to understand the question. After you hear the question, read the three possible answers and decide which one would be the best answer to the question you've heard. Listen to the following example.
    You'll hear:
      Is there a scenic drive to Hualien?
    You will read:
      (A) Sorry, I don't drive.
      (B) In my car.
      (C) Yes, take a right at the next corner, and
          go straight.
The best answer to the question "Is there a scenic drive to Hualien?" is (C) "Yes, take a right at the next corner, and go straight." Therefore you should choose answer (C) and mark (C) as shown below:
      (A)   (B)   (C)

1. (A) I went there to study last week.
   (B) Yes, geography's my favorite subject.
   (C) No, that's why I know all of these place names.

2. (A) A jet.
   (B) It's a prop plane.
   (C) Neither. It's a propeller plane.

3. (A) For thirty minutes.
   (B) In thirty minutes.
   (C) It didn't.

4. (A) No, I wouldn't. I hate coffee.
   (B) Yes, I do.
   (C) Sure. But tea.

5. (A) About three or four times a season.
   (B) It's once a month.
   (C) For a week.

6. (A) I don't too.
   (B) No, she does.
   (C) No, she doesn't.

7. (A) There it is.
   (B) Looks like it.
   (C) Not at all.

8. (A) Yes, they are. They need being shined.
   (B) Yes, they are. They need shining.
   (C) Yes, they are. They need shined.

9. (A) Yes, he is a child
   (B) Yes, he is my youngest one.
   (C) He is John.

10. (A) Yes, here you are.
    (B) I'll get you there.
    (C) I won't be long.

11. (A) Neither. She is a bookkeeper.
    (B) Yes, she is.
    (C) Either one will do.

12. (A) Yes. How do you think of that?
    (B) Yes. Why do you think that?
    (C) Yes. What do you think of that?

13. (A) No, thank you. I don't care for any just now.
    (B) Yes, I do. It's delicious, isn't it?
    (C) No, I'd like coffee, please.

14. (A) I don't mind.
    (B) I lost your phone.
    (C) I had no change.

15. (A) Yes, it's quite noisy.
    (B) Well, it's usually rather quiet.
    (C) Yes, it's quiet.

16. (A) I'm sorry, but they know I'm busy studying for a test.
    (B) Not yet, but I'm going to tomorrow.
    (C) Yes, I haven't had any time.

17. (A) Yes, I'd like to go but I'm busy.
    (B) Yes, I'm sorry to bother you.
    (C) No, I'm afraid I'll be too busy.

18. (A) Yes, I am.
    (B) Yes, this is she.
    (C) Yes, it is her. Who is this speaking?

19. (A) I prefer English.
    (B) I spent more time on mathematics.
    (C) We studied both.

20. (A) Yes, I would.
    (B) Here you are.
    (C) Here we are.

Part II

Directions: In this part of the test you will hear twenty
statements. Each statement will be spoken just once.
After you hear the statement, read the three sentences
and decide which one comes closest to the meaning of the
statement that you've heard. Listen to the following
example.

> You'll hear:
>   All three of them have $5.00.
> You will read:
>   (A) They have $15.00 in all.
>   (B) They have $20.00 in all.
>   (C) They have $10.00 in all.

Sentence (A) "They have $15.00 in all" means almost the
same as the statement you've heard "All three of them
have $5.00." Therefore you should choose answer (A).

21. (A) I decided to buy a new record.
    (B) I wanted to make a tape recording of the music.
    (C) The recording was not the one I wanted.

22. (A) Joanne worked in graduate school.
    (B) Joanne finished graduate school quickly.
    (C) Right after graduate school, Joanne started to
        work.

23. (A) Has he been to the library?
    (B) He needs a library card.
    (C) The librarian hasn't gotten there.

24. (A) I didn't know where you lived, so I didn't visit you.
    (B) I couldn't find your dress.
    (C) I had no idea you were visiting.

25. (A) He gradually learned to cook.
    (B) He can cook small meals.
    (C) He taught children how to cook.

26. (A) We have plenty of time to read the newspapers.
    (B) We won't be able to look at all the papers.
    (C) We don't have enough paper.

27. (A) I think that suit is too informal.
    (B) I think you should wear a warmer coat today.
    (C) I dont't think that coat is appropriate for the weather.

28. (A) Peter and I still have to buy our books.
    (B) Peter doesn't have his books, but I have mine.
    (C) Neither Peter nor I have studied yet.

29. (A) She is probably eating lunch with Linda.
    (B) She has to make Linda's lunch for her.
    (C) She must go to see Linda before lunch.

30. (A) Jim did some schoolwork at home.
    (B) Jim cleaned up the living room.
    (C) Jim rearranged the books in his study.

31. (A) She stopped to drink some coffee.
    (B) She couldn't find any coffee to drink.
    (C) She no longer drinks coffee.

32. (A) This morning I woke up after 7:30.
    (B) My alarm clock did not work this morning.
    (C) This morning I woke up at 7:30, but I usually wake up earlier.

33. (A) If we go on vacation, Mary will stay at our house.
    (B) After we return from vacation, we are going to buy a dog.
    (C) Mary will take care of our dog while we are on a vacation.

34. (A) John arrived at 9:00.
    (B) John arrived at 8:00.
    (C) John should have arrived at 8:00, but he didn't.

35. (A) The game of golf is very popular in Scotland.
    (B) The game of golf originated in the United States, but now it is more popular in Scotland.
    (C) The game of golf originated in Scotland, but now it is more popular in the United States.

36. (A) I saw my aunt and uncle thirteen years ago.
    (B) I haven't seen my aunt and uncle for thirty years.
    (C) I see my aunt and uncle once every thirteen years.

37. (A) He puts only sugar in his coffee.
    (B) There isn't enough sugar in his coffee.
    (C) He likes sugar, but the coffee he is drinking has too much.

38. (A) Arnold was embarrassed because his date wanted to pay for her own meal.
    (B) Arnold had less than $15.
    (C) Arnold didn't want to pay for his date's meal.

39. (A) George didn't have $1,000 for the man.
    (B) George wanted more than $1,000 for the man.
    (C) George agreed to take $1,000 for his car.

40. (A) Harvey turned around to answer the teacher's question.
    (B) Harvey must have been embarrassed.
    (C) Harvey looked in the red book for the answer to the question.

Part III

Directions: In this part of the test, you will hear ten short conversations between two speakers. At the end of each conversation, a third voice will ask a question about what was said. The question will be spoken just once. After you hear the conversation and the question about it, read the three possible answers and decide which one would be the best answer to the question you've heard. Listen to the following example:

You will hear:
   Man: Would you like to own your own business?
   woman: I wouldn't mind a bit.
   3rd voice: What did the woman mean?
You will read:
   (A) She couldn't make up her mind.
   (B) She doesn't have time for a job.
   (C) She'd like to have a company of her own.

From the conversation, we know that the woman would like to have her own company. The best answer, then is (C), "She would like to have a company of her own." Therefore you should choose answer (C).

41. (A) That he sees a nice motorcycle.
    (B) That motorcycles look nicer than cars.
    (C) That motorcycles can be dangerous.

42. (A) $20.00.   (B) $4.00.   (C) $10.00.

43. (A) In the lab.   (B) Eating lunch.
    (C) At home.

44. (A) Blue.   (B) Brown.   (C) Black.

45. (A) 8:50.   (B) 7:30.   (C) 8:00.

46. (A) Three.   (B) Five.   (C) Two.

47. (A) His wife doesn't want him to.
    (B) He has to work.
    (C) He will be out of town.

48. (A) He's wearing them.
    (B) On the cabinet.
    (C) Upstairs.

49. (A) 9:30.   (B) 10:30.   (C) 9:00.

50. (A) In a drugstore.   (B) At home.
    (C) In a doctor's office.

聽力測驗實況練習解答

Part I

【原文】　　　　　　　　　　　　　　　　　　　**【答案】**

1. Do you study a lot of geography on your own?　（B）
2. Is it a jet or a prop plane?　（A）
3. When will flight 103 leave for Munich?　（B）
4. Would you like a cup of coffee?　（A）
5. How often do you go skiing?　（A）

6. Doesn't Mary speak French?　（C）
7. What's wrong? Are we out of gas?　（B）
8. His shoes are dirty, aren't they?　（B）
9. Is this your son?　（B）
10. Could you reach me that dictionary?　（A）

11. Is she a secretary or a typist?　（A）
12. I hear you got 100% on your English test.　（C）
13. Would you like some coffee?　（A）
14. Why didn't you phone me from the station when you arrived?　（C）
15. Is your hometown quiet or noisy?　（B）

16. Haven't you written to your family this week?　（B）
17. Can you come over for supper tomorrow?　（C）
18. Hello. Is this Nancy?　（B）
19. Which did you study harder, English or mathematics?　（B）

20. Would you pass me the mustard? **（B）**

【註釋】

1. *on one's own* 獨自地；獨立地　　5. go skiing 滑雪
7. *out of gas* 沒有汽油了　　Looks like it. 看起來好像是。
10. reach〔ritʃ〕*vt.* 把（某物）遞給（某人）
13. *care for* 喜歡　　20. mustard〔'mʌstəd〕*n.* 芥末

Part Ⅱ

【原文】　　　　　　　　　　　　　　　　　　　　　　【答案】

21. I wanted to record the music. **（B）**

22. Joanne finished graduate school and got a job
immediately. **（C）**

23. He has to get a library card, doesn't he? **（B）**

24. If I'd known your address, I would have visited you. **（A）**

25. Little by little, he learned to cook. **（A）**

26. We haven't got enough time to check all these papers. **（B）**

27. Do you think that coat is suitable to wear on such
a hot day? **（C）**

28. I haven't bought my books yet and neither has Peter. **（A）**

29. She must have gone to Linda's for lunch. **（A）**

30. Jim read a book and did some studying in the living
room? **（A）**

31. My sister stopped drinking coffee. **（C）**

32. I usually wake up at 7:30, but this morning I over-
slept. **（A）**

33. While we're on vacation, Mary will look after the dog. (**C**)

34. John was supposed to be here at 8 o'clock, but he's late. (**C**)

35. Although the game of golf originated in Scotland. it is probably more popular in the United States than anywhere else. (**C**)

36. It's been thirty years since I have seen my aunt and uncle. (**B**)

37. He likes sugar in his coffee, but nothing else. (**A**)

38. Arnold was embarrassed to tell his date that he didn't have $15 to pay for the meal. (**B**)

39. The man offered $1,000 for the car, but George shook his head. (**B**)

40. Harvey's face turned bright red when the teacher asked him a question. (**B**)

【註釋】

25. ***little by little*** 逐漸地＝ gradually

37. ***nothing else*** 沒有別的了   39. ***shake one's head*** 搖頭表不贊同

Part Ⅲ

【原文】   【答案】

41. *Woman*: Be careful. That car is coming very fast.

  Man: You have to keep an eye out for motor-cycles.

  3rd voice : What does the man mean? (**C**)

42. **Man**: The pants are $10.00 and the shirt is $6.00.

Woman: Here's a twenty-dollar bill.

3rd voice: How much change will the woman get? (**B**)

43. **Woman**: Hello, Mr. Jones. This is Betty Smith. May I speak to my husband?

Man: John is in the lab now, Betty. And then he's going to eat lunch. I'll tell him to call you at home.

3rd voice: Where is the woman's husband? (**A**)

44. **Man**: I really like this black necktie.

Woman: But the blue or gold one will look much nicer with your brown suit.

3rd voice: What color necktie does the man want? (**C**)

45. **Woman**: I wonder if John will be here by 8:00. He's supposed to be.

Man: His wife said he left at 7:30, so he should be here by 8:15 at the latest.

3rd voice: What time is John supposed to arrive? (**C**)

46. **Man**: Henry has four classes on Wednesday and Peter has three.

Woman: I only have two, but I have five on Thursday.

3rd voice: How many classes does Peter have on Wednesday? (**A**)

47. *Woman* : Are you going to the Johnson's party tomorrow night?

   Man : I don't think so. I have to work and my wife will be out of town.

   3rd voice : Why isn't the man going to the party? （**B**）

48. *Man* : I was wearing my glasses a little while ago, but now I can't find them.

   Woman : They must be upstairs because they aren't on the table or cabinet.

   3rd voice : Where are the man's glasses? （**C**）

49. *Woman* : Have you seen Mr. O'Hara? He usually is here by 9:00.

   man : He said he was coming at 9:30 today, but it's already 10:00. I wonder where he is.

   3rd voice : What time does Mr. O'Hara usually come? （**C**）

50. *Man* : Can you tell me where to find aspirin?

   Woman : That will be in the third aisle to your left.

   3rd voice : Where did this conversation probably take place? （**A**）

【註釋】

41. ***keep an eye out for*** 警戒

48. cabinet〔'kæbənɪt〕*n.* 櫥櫃

50. aisle〔aɪl〕*n.* 狹長的通道；走廊

3 如何準備英語口試

唸英文短句測發音
中英口譯考反應力
問答題涵蓋一般／專業知識

唸英文短句測發音

導遊身負傳達的重任。如果因為**發音不清楚或不正確**,觀光客不但聽不懂,**甚至可能誤解**,而造成不良的後果。所以這是觀光局舉辦導遊甄試時,不得不慎重考核的原因。

畢竟,這項考試旨在測驗考生應用英語的**條件與能力**,所以重點雖是**測發音**,但決非考專門性的語言學。因此,讀者準備的重點不外乎**咬字正確、發音清楚、抓準音調**。以下是幾項常混淆的發音,應多加注意,並常常練習。

1. /θ/ 和 /s/ 如:th_ink, s_ink
2. /ʃ/ 和 /tʃ/ 如:wa_sh, wa_tch
3. /l/ 和 /r/ 如:l_ight, r_ight
4. /ε/ 和 /e/ 如:p_epper, p_aper
5. /ε/ 和 /æ/ 如:p_en, p_an
6. /o/ 和 /ɔ/ 如:c_old, c_aught
7. /ʌ/ 和 /ɑ/ 如:c_up, c_op
8. /ɚ/ 和 /ə/ 如:broth_er, sof_a

現在,請跟著錄音帶,**將下面的短句唸熟**,口試就不難過關了!

短句練習：

1. Lenny learned languages and law in the library.

2. Three thousand three hundred thirty-three.

3. The view was beautiful beyond belief.

4. Who'd be fooled with such food?

5. I think the boat will sink.

6. The boss had a bath and then took the bus to the base.

7. Sally sings songs while sitting in the shade at the seashore.

8. The jogger was shocked when John shouted at Tom.

9. They went further and further over there.

10. The girls hurried to the jeweler with their earrings.

11. Four firemen fought the fire for four hours.

12. Sam sat down and had half a ham sandwich.

13. They sang several sad songs.

14. They began going with the gang.

15. Chris sells cloth for shorts, shirts and pants.

16. I hope you will be happy.

17. How do you feel today?

18. I'm glad you could come.

19. How do you eat this?

20. What is this for?

21. Will you pass me the salt, please?

22. What do you recommend?

23. Where can I leave my coat?

24. Everything was so delicious.

25. Would you like to have some more?

26. Excuse me. I didn't quite catch your name.

27. Would you mind speaking more slowly?

28. That's up to you to decide.

29. Hold still a moment while I focus the camera.

30. How late are you open on weekdays?

31. On what floor is the childrens' wear department?

32. Do you have the same style in another color?

33. What material is it made of?

34. I don't see anything I'd really like to buy here.

35. Don't you have anything cheaper?

36. Can you give me a better price?

37. We'd like a table near the window.

38. How much is the admission fee?

39. What's the round-trip fare?

40. We must be off early tomorrow morning.

41. I'm packed and all set to go.

42. You've a good sense of humor.

43. You've been a big help.

44. That's why I must stay with you.

45. I think you better do it yourself.

46. Stick around for a couple of minutes.

47. Could you spare me a minute, please?

48. How does that sound to you?

49. Why don't you come with us?

50. Anything else you want?

Se Habla Español

② 中英口譯考反應力

導遊在帶團旅遊的當中，常常會碰到須將國人的意思轉達給外國觀光客的場合，所以**敏捷的口譯能力**決不可少。

由於須口譯的時機通常不容許停頓或吞吞吐吐，因此您首先要具備的條件是「**反應迅速**」。然而，要達到臨場反應迅速的境界，端賴平時不斷訓練。何況，口譯的題目通常並不難，且大部分與日常生活有關。因此您所要做的，只是讓自己「習慣」用**耳聽、口傳**的方式，表達原本就會說的英語。

要達到「習慣」（即反應快）的境界，應配合下列幾項要點：

1. **用英語思考**（Think in English）。
2. **時時刻刻將聽到的字句、看到的事物，在心中譯成英語。**

平時如能採用這兩項方法訓練，到須要口譯的時候，就能省掉在腦中「**中→英，英→中**」的程序，而能夠很直接的**脫口而出**。

以下列出英語導遊在各種場合可能碰到的口譯句子，請讀者務必自己先試著譯，然後再核對後面的解答。

中→英 口譯練習

1. 我要買一張本市的觀光地圖。

I want to buy a tourist map of this city.

2. 要我帶你到處逛逛嗎？

Shall I show you around?

3. 你要在台灣待多久？

How long will you stay in Taiwan?

4. 台灣有什麼使你印象最深刻？

What impressed you the most about Taiwan?

5. 別錯過故宮博物院。

Don't miss the National Palace Museum.

6. 希望你在台灣停留的期間很愉快。

I hope you enjoyed your stay in Taiwan.

7. 我能看看你的護照，以確定身份嗎？

May I see your passport for identification?

8. 我們不收私人支票。

We don't accept any personal checks.

9. 每天下午都有一趟遊覽，兩點鐘從這裏出發。

There's a tour every afternoon, leaving here at two o'clock.

10. 你比較喜歡看什麼？

Which would you prefer to see?

11. 這整組不分開賣。

We can't break up the set.

12. 請你在這裏簽名好嗎？

May I have your signature right here?

13. 你必須先申請。

Your must apply for it first.

14. 請你在後面背書好嗎？

Would you endorse on the back, please?

15. 你願意跟我站在一起照張相嗎？

Would you stand with me to have a picture taken?

16. 你的領帶有一點歪。

Your tie is a little crooked.

17. 抱歉，你得排隊。

I'm sorry. You'll have to get in line.

18. 你要加那種調味料？

What kind of dressing would you like?

19. 你要甜點嗎？

Would you like some dessert?

20. 那樣對你方便嗎？

Will that be convenient for you?

21. 如果你想要的話，我們可以幫你預約。

If you wish, we could make reservations for you.

22. 你什麼時候要離開？

When would you like to leave?

23. 這東西正在大拍賣。

This is on sale.

24. 坐計程車要十分鐘。

It's 10 minutes by taxi.

25. 在那棟樓的後面。

It's in the back of the building.

26. 在反方向。

It's in the opposite direction.

27. 到那裏最好的辦法是坐火車。

The best way to get there is by train.

28. 在台北車站換車。

Change at Taipei Station.

29. 請填好這張卡片。　　　　　　Please fill in this card.

30. 我們今晚有一個歡迎會。　　　We're having a welcome party tonight.

31. 我們可以給你特價。　　　　　We can make a special discount.

32. 外面有車在等你。　　　　　　There's a car waiting for you outside.

33. 他們會來車站接我們。　　　　They'll pick us up at the station.

34. 他們都是專業人員。　　　　　They're all professionals.

35. 你要住那一家飯店？　　　　　What hotel are you staying at?

36. 你的咖啡要不要加糖？　　　　Do you want some sugar in your coffee?

37. 這裏沒有叫哈洛（Harold）的人。　There's no Harold here.

38. 你要不要留話？　　　　　　　Would you like to leave your message?

39. 火車多久一班？　　　　　　　How often do the trains run.

40. 一直坐到這條路線的終點站。　Just ride to the end of the line.

③ 問答題涵蓋一般／專業知識

英語導遊口試的**第 3 項**是20題問答。其中有**10 題是簡答**，另外**10 題是詳答**。雖然只要區區20題，其可能考的範圍，必涵蓋英語導遊必備的常識，而且不論深淺。所以，您除了一般性的**生活會話**要能運用自如之外，對於深入介紹地理、風景、歷史、文化等**專業知識**，更要能勝人一籌，才有能力讓觀光客覺得不虛此行。

由於出題範圍相當廣泛，如果草率猜題應付，很難穩操勝算。因此，我們將簡答和詳答常考的內容，各分為**5 個 Groups**，讓您先有整體的概念。每個 Group 收錄**具代表性且常考**的問題和**完整正確**的解答，總共180題。練習時，務必配合錄音帶，才有「**實況**」的效果。

Part Ⅰ**簡答題**： Group 1　　Personal Information 個人資料

Group 2　　General Information 台灣概況

Group 3　　Tour Sites 觀光勝地

Group 4　　History and Culture 歷史與文化

Group 5　　Taipei 台北

Part Ⅱ**詳答題**： Group 1　　General Information 台灣概況

Group 2　　Tour Sites 觀光勝地

Group 3　　History 歷史

Group 4　　Culture 文化

Group 5　　Taipei 台北

Part Ⅰ　Group 1　Personal Information 個人資料

1. Are you the youngest child in your family?

No, I'm right in the middle, number 2 of 3.

2. How many brothers and sisters do you have?

I have two brothers and one sister.

3. Have you ever been abroad?

Yes. My parents took my brother and me to Europe when I was twelve years old.

4. Where's your favorite place on Taiwan?

It would have to be my home town, Cheng Kung, on Taiwan's east coast.

5. Do you have any relatives overseas?

Yes, my younger brother is studying in America.

6. Why did you become a tour guide?

I like people, and take pride in showing the beauty of my country to foreign guests.

7. Have you been everywhere on the island?

I've been to most of the tourist attractions, but there are still many place I have yet to see.

8. Where did you go to college?

I graduated from Cheng Kung University's Department of Foreign Languages.

9. Are you a Taiwanese or a mainlander?

Both, actually. My mother is from Shanghai, and my father was born and raised in Taichung.

10. How did your English get to be so good?

I studied English hard ever since junior high, and have listened to ICRT every day for the last six years.

Group 2 General Information 台灣概況

11. What are Taiwan's length and width?

The island of Taiwan is 394 kilometers (236 miles) long and 144 kilometers (86 miles) at its widest.

12. How much of Taiwan's land surface is arable?

Between 24 and 31 percent is arable.

13. Where is most of the arable land?

It is on the western coastal plain, where most all of the nation's rice is grown.

14. What is the population of Taiwan, and what's the growth rate?

Taiwan presently has 19.5 million people, and the population growth rate in 1985 was 1.84.

15. What is the population density in Taiwan?

It is the world's second highest at slightly over 500 persons per square kilometer.

** arable 〔ˈærəbl〕 *adj.* 適於耕種的   population density "人口密度"

16. Do you get snow in Taiwan?

Only on a few mountains: Ho Huan Shan, Yu Shan and Yangmingshan.

17. When are typhoons most likely to come?

They only come during the period from June to October. We usually get at least one or two a year.

18 Do typhoons do much damage?

Some do and some don't. Last year's Typhoon Wayne wrought havoc, but the later Abbey did little damage.

19. Do you get a lot of earthquakes in Taiwan?

We get several thousand a year, but only a few of them are noticeable.

20. What is the highest mountain in Taiwan, and how high is it?

The tallest is Yushan (Jade Mountain) at nearly 4,000 meters (13,200 feet).

21. How many temples are there in Taiwan?

There are approximately 5,000 temples, or one for every four thousand people.

22. Is there a state religion of the R.O.C.?

No. Religious freedom is guaranteed by the constitution.

23. Does Kaohsiung have as serious a pollution problem as Taipei?

No, though there are times when cement dust from the numerous nearby cement factories seriously pollutes the air.

24. Is there only one Confucian temple in Taiwan?

No, there are, in fact, ten of them, scattered throughout the island.

25. How many aborigines are there on Taiwan?

There are approximately 300,000 of them, divided among 9 tribes.

26. What does it mean that Taipei and Kaohsiung are "special municipalities"?

This means that they each enjoy the status of a province, and each's mayor likewise the status of a provincial governor.

27. How many Buddhists are there on Taiwan?

There were 810,000 registered Buddhists in 1986, but the actual number is probably in the millions.

** aborigines 〔͵æbə'rɪdʒə͵niz〕 *n*. 原始的居民
   municipality 〔͵mjunɪsə'pælətɪ〕 *n*. 自治市（區）
   status 〔'stetəs〕 *n*. 身份；地位

28. **Where is the seat of the Taiwan Provincial Government?**

It is at Chunghsing Village, just a half hour's drive from Taichung.

Group 3　Tour Sites觀光勝地

29. **Where is Keelung?**

On the north coast, about 40 minutes from Taipei by bus.

30. **How many days a year does it rain in Keelung?**

It rains there on the average of 214 days a year, and as such is one of the wettest cities of the world.

31. **Is Kaohsiung a seaport?**

Yes, it is the largest in Taiwan, in fact, and one of the busiest and sizable ports in the world.

32. **How many pieces of art does the National Palace Museum possess?**

There are some 625,000 pieces that belong to the National Palace Museum.

33. **What is the Window on Cathay?**

Known by many other names as well, it is an outdoor display of miniatures of 68 famous structures or construction projects in mainland China and Taiwan.

** miniature〔ˊmɪnɪətʃɚ〕*n.* 縮小之物

34. Is the National Museum of History worth a visit?

Yes, it contains over 10,000 art pieces, some nearly 4,000 years old. Its bronze collection is especially extensive.

35. What is the big park behind the National Museum of History in Taipei?

That is the Taiwan Provincial Botanical Garden, which contains 700 species of plants. Vegetation from tropical, sub-tropical and temperate zones is represented.

36. What is the tribe of aborigines that inhabits Wulai?

They are the Atayal, the second largest of Taiwan's aboriginal tribes.

37. How many miniature people figures are there at the Window on Cathay exhibit?

There are 50,000, of the average 6.8 centimeters (2.7 inch) tall figures. They are one twenty-fifth the size of human beings.

38. Is the Shimen Reservoir natural or man-made?

It is man-made, constructed from 1956 to 1964 at a cost of US$85 million.

** bronze〔brɑnz〕*n.* 青銅　　botanical〔boˊtænɪkḷ〕*adj.* 植物的

39. Where and what is Peitou?

It is north-northwest of Taipei, about a half hour away; it is a resort town used by the Japanese as a hot springs spa.

40. What is Snake Alley?

It is properly called Huahsi Street, in Taipei, and is a lane where tens of snake merchants perform with, slaughter and serve meals of poisonous snakes.

41. What is there to do at Pitan?

There are gondolas and rowboats for rent, and you can swim anywhere in the lake. Cross the suspension bridge and walk through a beautiful Air Force cemetary.

42. How long is the Penghu Bay Bridge?

Including its approaches and dikes, it is 5,541 meters (6,060 yards) long. Its overwater section is 2,160 meters (2,362 yards) long.

43. How many islands are there in the Penghu Archipelago?

There are 64 islands in the archipelago, and their total area is 126.8 square kilometers(49 square miles).

44. Is Penghu County heavily populated?

No, but neither is it sparsely populated, as 120,000 people inhabit it.

** spa〔spɑ;spɔ〕*n.* 溫泉（名勝）　　sparsely〔'spɑrslɪ〕*adv.* 稀疏地
archipelago〔ˌɑrkə'pɛləˌgo〕*n.* 列島

45. **Are all of the Penghu islands inhabited?**

No, only 43 of them are inhabited, and over half of the population lives in Makung, the county seat.

46. **Is Orchid Island (Lanyu) inhabited?**

Yes, it is inhabited by the Yami, the smallest of Taiwan's 9 tribes of aborigines.

47. **Where and how large is Orchid Island?**

It is 76 kilometers (47½ miles) southeast of Taitung, a city on Taiwan's southeastern coast. It is 27 square kilometers (10 ½ square miles) in area.

48. **Have the Yami all been assimilated into the Chinese culture?**

No. They still retain their own customs, for the most part, but the younger people have received a standard education.

49. **How long has the Kenting Forest Recreation Area been open?**

It opened in 1906 with the name, "The Kenting Tropical Botanical Garden."

50. **What is the elevation at Sun Moon Lake?**

Sun Moon Lake is 762 meters (2,500 feet) above sea level.

** assimilate 〔ə'sɪmḷet〕 v. 同化

51. How can I get to Sun Moon Lake from Taipei?

You can either take a bus from Taipei directly there, or take the train (or a bus) to Taichung, and catch the bus to Sun Moon Lake at the Taichung Bus Station.

52. What special sights are there at Sun Moon Lake?

The lake itself is a splendid sight, but in addition there are two reknowned temples and a famous pagoda there.

53. What's famous about Lukang?

It's famous primarily for its distinctive temples and Folk Arts Museum, but also for its residents' recent rejection of the construction there of a Du Pont factory.

54. How long is the East-West Cross-Island Highway?

The total length of the two branches is 347 kilometers (215 miles).

55. Does the East-West Cross-Island Highway pass through Taroko Gorge?

Yes. The road through Taroko is the easternmost section of the highway, just inland from Hualien.

56. Is the Alishan alpine railway electric, like the main railroad?

No. It is a narrow-gauge railway, and the trains that run on it are diesel-powered.

57. Is there a Southern Cross-Island Highway?

Yes, and some believe it to be even more spectacular than the Central Cross-Island Highway.

Group 4 History and Culture 歷史與文化

58. When did the Japanese occupy Taiwan?

They controlled Taiwan from from 1895 to 1945. Taiwan was returned to the R.O.C. following the Japanese surrender of World War II.

59. Who was Dr. Sun Yat-sen?

He was the Father of the Republic of China, whose thoughts form the basis of this constitutional democracy.

60. How long ago did the late President Chiang Kai-shek die?

He died on April, 1975 after having acted for nearly 35 years as president.

61. Who was Koxinga?

He was the Ming loyalist general who recaptured Taiwan from the Dutch in 1661.

62. Who was Wu Feng?

He was responsible for ending the aborigines' head-hunting practice, and so is a local hero (and god).

** recapture〔rɪˈkæptʃɚ〕 *v.* 收復

63. **Are there any historical government buildings in Taiwan?**

Yes, but they're few. One of them is in Taipei, at the botanical garden, and is called the Hsun Fu Yamen. It was built in 1887.

64. **What does a city god do?**

The city god and goddess protect the inhabitants of their city, guarding against attacks and epidemics. They also care for the dead.

65. **When was the beginning of the Republic of China?**

It was in 1911, when the Wu Chang Uprising successfully overthrew the Manchu Ching government.

66. **When did the Spanish occupy parts of Taiwan?**

They occupied Keelung and the northern coastline from 1626 to 1642, when the Dutch forced them out.

67. **How long were the Dutch here?**

They arrived in 1624, occupied primarily portions of northern Taiwan, and left after Koxinga (Cheng Cheng Kung) defeated them in 1661.

68. **How do heroes become gods?**

The Chinese are lavish in their praise for their predecessors. A hero or heroine becomes popular with the people, and upon his or her death is enshrined.

** lavish 〔'lævɪʃ〕 *adj.* 過度的　enshrine 〔rɪ'ʃraɪn〕 *v.* 奉祀於廟堂之中
predecessor 〔,prɛdɪ'sɛsɚ〕 *n.* 祖先

69. **When were French troops in Taiwan?**

They were here for eight months- in Keelung- in 1894. They had originally planned to occupy Taiwan and the Pescadores.

70. **Were there any rebellions during Japan's occupation of Taiwan?**

Yes, countless small rebellions, especially during the early years of the occupation. In 1930 some 3,000 aborigines made the last large protest, and were slaughtered.

71. **When is the Month of Ghosts?**

It is the seventh lunar month, usually falling sometime around mid August to mid September on the Gregorian calendar.

Group 5 Taipei 台北

72. **How tall is the Chiang Kai - shek Memorial Hall?**

It is 70 meters (229.6 feet) tall, which would be roughly equivalent to 23 stories.

73. **How old is the Taipei Lungshan temple?**

The present structure has stood since 1959; it is the fifth structure at that site with that name.

74. **How large is Taipei?**

In terms of population, 2.5 million; in terms of area, 272 square kilometers (105 square miles).

** Pescadores 〔 ˌpɛskɑˈdɔrɪz 〕 *n.* 澎湖群島

75. How many ports serve Taipei?

Two airports, the CKS International and the Sungshan domestic, and one seaport, Keelung.

76. Has Taipei always been the capital of Taiwan?

No, Tainan was the capital for 203 years, from 1684 to 1887.

77. Is there a beach near Taipei?

There are popular ocean beaches near Taipei, on the north coast. They are Chinshan, Paishawan (White Sand Bay) Beach, Green Bay, and Fulung.

78. When did Taipei become the capital of Taiwan?

Taipei became the capital of Taiwan in 1887. It replaced Tainan in this capacity.

79. Where can I shop in Taipei?

The Wanhwa District and neighborhood night markets are good for food, trinkets, books, etc., but for more durable goods you should go to department stores.

80. When did Taipei become the capital of the R.O.C.?

It became the R.O.C.'s provisional capital in 1949, after the government's retreat from the mainland.

Part II Group 1 General Information 台灣概況

1. How large is Taiwan? What are its main geographical features?

Geographically, it is 394 kilometers long (200 miles) and 144 kilometers (86 miles) at its widest. The total area of all of the islands comprising Taiwan Province is roughly 36,000 square kilometers, or about 13,850 square miles. Taiwan proper is shaped like a tobacco leave, its poles pointing northeast and southwest. Approximately two thirds of the island's surface is mountainous.

2. Why do so many place names in Taiwan start with " tai "?

In these names " tai " represents " Taiwan, " and the latter portion of each word indicates location : Middle, north, south, east and west Taiwan, all names of cities excluding " west Taiwan, " are Taichung, Taipei, Tainan, Taitung and Taihsi, respectively.

3. What are the outlying islands that help comprise Taiwan Province?

Taiwan Province is 77 islands, 64 of which form the Penghu Archipelago, the chain which lies between Taiwan island and the mainland coast. Other noteworthy islands include Orchid and Green islands off the southeastern coast, and Shia Liu Chiu, in the Taiwan Straits just south of Kaohsiung.

** comprize 〔kəm'praɪz〕 *vt*. 構成
   exclude 〔ɪk'sklud〕 *v*. 除去   orchid 〔'ɔrkɪd〕 *n*. 蘭

4. What is Taiwan's climate like?

It is subtropical, for the most part, with northern and southern average annual temperatures at 21.7℃（71.2℉） and 24.1℃（75.7℉）, respectively. Winters and springs are rainy and cool in the North, and hot and extremely dry in the South. Summers bring much-needed showers to the South and intense heat and humidity to the North.

5. When is the typhoon season? Do typhoons cause much damage?

It usually begins in mid-June and lasts through October in some years. We normally get typhoons every year, and they cause considerable damage to homes, crops, roads and other communication lines. Last year's（1986）Typhoon Wayne caused 63 people's deaths and did NT＄14.2 billion worth of damage.

6. How far is Taiwan from Mainland China?

Taiwan proper lies only 160 kilometers — 96 miles — from the coast of Fukien Province on Mainland China. R.O.C. — controlled Matzu and Chinmen islands, however, are within sight of the mainland.

**　subtropical〔sʌb'trɑpɪkl̩〕*adj.* 亞熱帶的
　　humidity〔hju'mɪdətɪ〕*n.* 濕氣；濕度；潮濕
　　considerable〔kən'sɪdərəbl̩〕*adj.* 不少（小）的；相當大（多）的
　　proper〔'prɑpə〕*adj.* 眞正的（通常用於名詞後）
　　within sight "在見得到的地方"

7. Aside from Shimen, what other reservoirs are there?

There are three other major reservoirs : Tzengwen, the largest reservoir in Taiwan ; Coral Lake, which feeds off Tzengwen ; and Cheng Ching Lake, just outside of Kaohsiung. Tzengwen was completed in 1973 at a cost of US$151 million, and took six years to build. Coral Lake is so called because it resembles a piece of coral when viewed from the air. Cheng Ching Lake is a favorite Kaohsiung tourist attraction.

8. What Chinese dialects do people in Taiwan speak?

The R.O.C.'s national language is, of course, Mandarin — the Peking dialect, but most people also speak Taiwanese, an offshoot of the Fukien dialect. Further, a relatively large Hakka-speaking group continues to thrive in parts of North and Central Taiwan. Other people speak Shanghaiese, Amoy, and Cantonese, to name a few, but they are relatively few.

9. What are the most popular religions in Taiwan?

Chinese folk religion, a belief in a complex conglomeration of Buddhist, Taoist and Chinese folk gods, is easily the most popular. The most popular sects include those of the gods, Matzu and Kuan Yin. In addition, Christians number roughly 550,000 and Moslems 54,300.

** coral 〔'kɑrəl〕 *n*. 珊瑚　Mandarin〔'mændərɪn〕 *n*. 國語
offshoot〔'ɔf,ʃut ; 'ɑf-〕 *n*. 分枝　　Hakka〔'hɑk'kɑ〕 *n*.客家（人）
thrive〔θraɪv〕 *v*. 繁茂　　Amoy〔ə'mɔi〕 *n*. 廈門
conglomeration〔kən,glɑmə'reʃən〕 *n*.聚集
sect〔sɛkt〕 *n*.宗派 ; 黨派

10. What national parks does Taiwan have?

There are four national parks. Starting in the North, there is Mt. Yangming National Park, famous for its cherry and azalea blossoms in Spring. In Central Taiwan there is Taroko National Park, just inland from the eastern seashore. Taroko Gorge has been counted among the most beautiful natural sites on earth. Also in Central Taiwan is Yu Shan National Park, and at the very southern tip of the island is tropical Kenting National Park.

11. How many places on Taiwan can we fly to?

There are six civilian airports for domestic use on Taiwan island, at Taipei, Chiayi, Tainan, Kaohsiung, Taitung, and Hualien. In addition there are two international airports: the above-mentioned Kaohsiung airport, and the Chiang Kai-shek International Airport in Taoyuan. Not to be forgotten, there are also airports on Lanyu Island and at Makung, Penghu.

12. How many international seaports are there in Taiwan?

There are five : Kaohsiung, the largest; Keelung, the port serving Taipei; Suao, north of Hualien on the east coast; Taichung, the newest harbor; and Hualien, Taiwan's famous marble capital. In 1986, Kaohsiung became the second largest container port (in terms of volume) in the world.

** gorge 〔gɔrdʒ〕 *n.* 峽　　civilian 〔sə'vɪljən〕 *adj.* 民間的；平民的
marble 〔'mɑrbl〕 *n.* 大理石　　container 〔kən'tenɚ〕 *n.* 貨櫃

13. **Is there an international trade center in Taiwan?**

There are two, actually. One is the Export Products Display Center at the Song-shang Airport, which has 134 booths representing over 1,000 local manufacturers and traders. The other is the Taipei World Trade Center on Hsinyi Rd., an enormous complex that has become a major Western Pacific hub for international trade relations.

14. **How extensive is the railroad system in Taiwan?**

The main electric trunk railroad runs from Keelung in the North to Fangliao in the South, well beyond Kaohsiung. The eastern branch begins again in Keelung and extends to Taitung in the South. The Taitung-Pingtung link — now under construction — will then complete the system, joining the eastern and western lines.

15. **What must you declare when entering Taiwan?**

Dutiable articles, new articles, samples, machine parts and accessories, industrial and raw materials, instruments, apparatuses, hand tools, etc., and any bonded baggage, gold bars, weapons, radioactive substances, X-ray apparatuses and medicines. Forbidden articles include any item made in or exported from communist China, N. Korea, Vietnam, Cambodia, Albania, Romania, the U.S.S.R., and Cuba.

** complex〔'kɑmplɛks〕*n.*綜合物   booth〔buð;buθ〕*n.*商展等之攤位
hub〔hʌb〕*n.*中心   declare〔dɪ'klɛr〕*vt.*申報
dutiable〔'djutɪəbḷ〕*adj.*應納稅的
accessory〔æk'sɛsərɪ〕*n.*附屬品
apparatus〔ˌæpə'rætəs〕*n.*儀器；器械

16. For how long are tourist visas valid?

Tourist visas are valid for 6 months from the date of issue. They are good for a 2-month stay and may be extended twice for a total stay of 6 months. Besides tourist visas, transit visas are obtainable. They are valid for 3 months from the date of issue and good for 2-week stay, but they may not be extended.

17. What articles cannot be taken out of Taiwan?

Departing travelers are prohibited from carrying gold or silver bullion or bars, wheat and other grains, unauthorized reproductions of books and records, and weapons. Also, no genuine antiques or ancient coins or paintings may be taken out.

18. Are there any car rental agencies in Taiwan?

Yes, there are a handful of them, mostly catering to the local population. A few companies, though, welcome foreigners to rent from them, and will accept major foreign credit cards. Just this year the first foreign car rental agency opened offices all over the island, offering for the first time in Taiwan one-way rentals.

** visa〔ˋvizə〕*n.* 簽證　　valid〔ˋvælɪd〕*adj.* 依法有效的
issue〔ˋɪʃʊ〕*n.* 發行　　prohibit〔proˋhɪbɪt〕*vt.* 禁止
bullion〔ˋbʊljən〕*n.* 金塊；銀塊；金條；銀條
antique〔ænˋtik〕*n.* 古董　　cater〔ˋketə〕*vi.* 迎合
car rental agency 租車公司
rental〔ˋrɛntl〕*n.* 租金

19. **What do I do to get a mountain pass？**

They're sometimes very difficult to obtain, but you can apply at the Taiwan Provincial Police Department, or the Foreign Affairs Police in the county seat of the area in which you wish to climb. Obtaining a B-class pass is almost routine, but A-class passes — for foreign tourists — are next to impossible.

20. **Where can l go to receive acupuncture treatment？**

There are thousands of acupuncturists in Taiwan, and it's difficult to know who's for real and who's a quack. Your main concern in seeking an acupuncturist is sanitation. Therefore, insist that he or she use only disposable needles.

21. **Can I take antiques out of the country？**

No, not usually. It is illegal to sell or transfer pri-
vately owned antiques or ancient artifacts to aliens that wish to take the articles abroad. This includes any antiques, from coins to lamps to sculptures. In es-sence, nothing over 100 years old may be taken out of the country.

** **_mountain pass_** 入山證 **_next to impossible_** 幾乎不可能
quack〔kwæk〕*n.* 庸醫
acupuncture〔'ækjupʌŋktʃɚ〕*n.* 針灸
sanitation〔͵sænə'teʃən〕*n.* 衛生

22. **Is there any snow skiing in Taiwan?**

Yes, for a short period in the winter months, at Ho Huan Shan, about a four-hour drive from Taichung. Mind you, the skiing facilities can't compare with those of North American or European resorts, but it is still an enjoyable experience to go there.

23. **Can I play golf on Taiwan?**

Yes, there are about 20 large golf courses in Taiwan, and many more smaller ones, where you can enjoy a pleasant game. Taipei alone has eight courses. Taiwan's subtropical climate allows for year-round golfing.

24. **What are Taiwan's major national holidays?**

The major ones include Founders' Day on January 1, Tomb Sweeping Day (also the day of Chiang Kai-shek's death) on April 5, National Day on October 10, Birthday of Chiang Kai-shek (also Veterans Day) on October 31, Dr. Sun Yat-sen's Birthday on December 12, and Constitution Day on December 25.

25. **How can I exchange my N.T. for U.S. dollars when I leave Taiwan?**

You can only do that at an international port of entry and exit, the most common being, of course, the CKS International Airport. You must present your original exchange receipts that you received when you originally exchanged U.S. for N.T. dollars.

** resort〔rɪˈzɔrt〕*n.* 常去之處　　sub-tropical〔sʌbˈtrɑpɪkl〕*adj.* 亞熱帶的

Group 2 Tour Sites 觀光勝地

26. How can travellers get to Alishan?

To get to Alishan, travellers can take a diesel-powered train from Chiayi. The railway, crossing 77 bridges and passing through 50 tunnels, is about 72 kilometers long. It takes three and a half hours to get to the Alishan railway station, the highest station in East Asia. In addition to the railway, there is also the new highway linking Chiayi and Alishan.

27. What are the most spectacular natural scenes at Alishan?

One can see the Sacred Tree, a 3000-year-old cypress. Unfortunately, it was stricken dead by lightning in 1947. Also, from the observation deck atop a mountain peak, one can see the sunrise and the famous sea of clouds that rings Yushan, the loftiest peak in Northeast Asia.

28. What is so special about Kenting National Park?

Kenting National Park's 40,000 acres include about every form of scenic beauty known to man. The wildlife within the park is as varied as any over an equal area anywhere on earth. Moreover, more than 1,000 species of plants inhabit the park.

** diesel 〔ˈdizl̩〕 *n.* 柴油　　tunnel 〔ˈtʌnl̩〕 *n.* 隧道
spectacular 〔spɛkˈtækjələ〕 *adj.* 壯觀的
cypress 〔ˈsaɪprəs〕 *n.* 柏樹　　ring 〔rɪŋ〕 *vt.* 圍繞

29.Which god is enshrined in the Lungshan Temple?

Originally, the temple was dedicated to a Buddhist divinity Kuan Yin, the Goddess of Mercy, but now many other deities, including non-Buddhist ones, are enshrined there. The most notable among them is a Taoist divinity Matsu, the Goddess of the Sea and the Empress of Heaven.

30. Is the present Lungshan Temple the original structure?

No. The original structure, completed in 1740, was razed by an earthquake in 1817, and replaced by another that was destroyed again in a typhoon in 1867. Since then it has undergone two more complete transformations, the first in 1926 and the second in 1959.

31. Please introduce the East-West Cross-Island Highway briefly.

This Highway, which took 10,000 workers 46 months to build, was completed in 1960 at a cost of nearly US$11 million. Opening up the great Central Mountain Range that dominates Taiwan's geography, it is a highway of surpassing magnificence, sublime loveliness and awesome grandeur. It winds from Taroko Gorge in the East to Tung-shih in the west, covering a distance of 192.8 kilometers.

** enshrine〔ɪn'ʃraɪn〕*vt.* 奉祀於廟堂中
　　dedicate〔'dɛdə'ket〕*vt.* 供奉　　deity〔'diətɪ〕*n.* 神
　　divinity〔də'vɪnətɪ〕*n.* 神　　raze〔rez〕*vt.* 摧毀
　　magnificence〔mæg'nɪfəsns〕*n.* 華麗；堂皇
　　grandeur〔'grænʤɚ〕*n.* 莊嚴

32. What is Keelung known for ?

Keelung is the second largest of the five international seaports in Taiwan. It is situated on the north coast, overlooking the East China Sea. Apart from being the seaport serving Taipei, it is also the northern terminal of the National Chungshan (Sun Yat-sen) North-South Freeway and the electrified trunk railroad, both of which extend to Kaoshiung in Southwest Taiwan. Keelung is also the junction of two coastal and several other highways.

33. Where does the North Coast Highway start and end ?

The North Coast Highway leads northwest from Keelung along the East China Sea coast then swings southwestward along the Taiwan Strait to the small town of Tamsui, near Taipei.

34. What are some points of interst on a trip from Keelung to Tamsui?

Yehliu, which is noted for its rock formations fashioned by the elements through the ages, is eye-dazzling. There, in particular, is the Queen's head, which is always popular with photographers.

Green Bay is a beach resort with facilities. Water sports, camp sites, an amusement park, and beachside bungalows are among the amenities one finds there. Other beaches, including Chensan and Paishawan, are also popular.

** overlook 〔͵ovɚˊlʊk〕 *vt.* 俯瞰　　*apart from* "除了～之外"
swing 〔ˊswɪŋ〕 *vi.* 廻轉　eye-dazzling 〔ˊaɪ͵dæzlɪŋ〕 *adj.* 使人眼花撩亂的
resort 〔rɪˊzɔrt〕 *n.* 遊樂勝地　　bungalow 〔ˊbʌŋgə͵lo〕 *n.* 小屋
amenity 〔əˊmɛnətɪ〕 *n.* 〔*pl.*〕令人愉快的事物或環境

35. What is Wulai noted for?

It is noted for its mountain resort. It is a flourishing village inhabited by aborigines of the Atayal tribe, the second largest tribe in Tauian. The aborigines make and sell handicrafts. They also give lively song and dance shows. There is a hillside narrow-gauge rail line and a cableway to a hilltop park.

36. What are some places of interest in Taichung?

First, there is the Taiwan Provincial Government's Handicraft Exhibition Hall at Tsaotun. Then there is the Happy Buddha of Taichung, with a hollow interior that contains lounges, showrooms, offices, a library, and classrooms. Furthermore, Chungshan Park, in the center of downtown Taichung, is a pleasant stop for weary travellers.

37. What are some places of interest in the Sun Moon Lake area?

The Hsuan Tzang Temple, named after the celebrated priest of the Tang Dynasty, is a favorite for tourists. The huge Wen-Wu or Literature-Warrior temple, dedicated to the sage Confucius as the Master of the Pen and to Kuan Ti, God of war, as the Master of the sword, is an interesting stop.

** flourishing〔ˈflɝɪʃɪŋ〕*adj.* 繁盛的

　aborigine〔ˌæbəˈrɪdʒəni〕*n.* 原始居民

　gauge〔gedʒ〕*n.* 軌幅　　lounge〔laʊndʒ〕*n.* 休息室

　warrior〔ˈwɔrɪɚ〕*n.* 戰士

38. What does "Yangming" mean, and what is there at Mt. Yangming Park?

The name "Yangming" was given to the park by the late President Chiang Kai-shek, after a 16th Century philosopher, Wang Yang-ming, whom he greatly admired. The park is famous for its cherry and azalea blossoms, which visitors may view in the early spring.

39. What is there to know about the Shimen Reservoir?

This 8 square kilometer (3 square mile) man-made lake lies snugly in the foothills of Snow Mountain, about 52 kilometers (32.6 miles) southwest of Taipei. Tourists can rent boats and fish there, and enjoy aborigine dance performances on Fairy Island in the middle of the reservoir. If Shimen doesn't whet your appetite, then you can also tour the nearby Window on China complex and the Leofoo Safari Park.

40. What is there to see at Lukang?

Deer Harbor, as its name reads in English, is a cultural goldmine, and is one of Taiwan's oldest towns. It is second only to Tainan in the member of temples that grace its streets. Its former Lungshan Temple was the oldest Buddhist temple on the island. The present temple was built in 1786. The Lukang Folk Arts Museum, housed in an elegant 60-year-old mansion, was opened in 1973, andrs offers intriguing displays.

** azalea〔əˈzeljə〕n. 杜鵑花   snugly〔ˈsnʌglɪ〕adv. 緊密地
intrigue〔ɪnˈtrig〕v. 引起…好奇和興趣

41. What is this Fokuang Shan place?

It is Taiwan's center of Buddhism, located about 35 kilometers (22 miles) north of Kaohsiung. Its name in English would be something like the Mountain of Buddha's Light. It is famous especially for its giant gold-colored gilded statue of Buddha, measuring 32 meters (105.6 feet) in height, and surrounded by 480 smaller statues each of 1.8 meters (6 feet) height.

42. Is Kaohsiung worth a visit?

By all means. The wide, tree-lined boulevards are welcome respite from the narrow, crowded, bustling streets of Taipei. Tourist sites abound, and include the Kaohsiung Fish Market on the wharf; Longevity Mountain Park near the top of a nearby mountain, from which is afforded a panoramic view of Kaohsiung and its busy harbor; and Cheng Ching Lake, where you can enjoy a full day's walk through a well-kept park.

43. How can I get to Penghu?

Several ways. You can get there by plane from Taipei, Tainan, Chiayi and Kaohsiung, or you can take the ferry from Kaohsiung. All flights and ferry land and docks at Makung, the capital of Penghu. Flights are quick and easy, but the 4 ½ - hour ferry ride is worth slowing down for.

** gilded 〔 'gɪldɪd〕 *adj.* 鍍金的；塗成金色的
boulevard 〔 'bulə,vɑrd；'bul-〕 *n.* 林蔭大道
panoramic 〔 ,pænə'ræmɪk〕 *adj.* 全景的
well-kept 〔 'wɛl 'kɛpt〕 *adj.* 照料得很好的；保管妥當的
ferry 〔 'fɛrɪ 〕 *n.* 渡船；渡口

44. What's the point of going all the way out to Penghu?

Penghu is truly a maritime community, unlike anything on Taiwan proper. It is interesting to note how the lifestyle here differs from those on Taiwan. Still, if you're more interested in tourist attractions, you won't be disappointed. For instance, Penghu is the site of the longest interisland bridge in East Asia: It is 2,160 meters (2,362 yards) long, and 5,541 meters (6,060 yards) long when its approaches and dikes are included in the calculation.

45. What other tourist sites are there at Penghu?

If you're looking for temples, then Penghu won't let you down, as it has 147 of them. The oldest one was built in 1593 to Matzu, Goddess of the Sea. Then there is the 300-year-old banyan tree supported by 700 square meter (7,535 square foot) latticed roof. Further, on the island of Chimei (seven Beauties) is the Tomb of the Seven Virgins, erected in honor of seven chaste beauties who drowned themselves there rather than allow a band of marauding pirates to ravage them.

46. Please give me a brief description of Tainan.

Tainan is Taiwan's oldest city, and served as its capital for 203 years, from 1684 to 1887. Koxinga (Cheng

---

** maritime 〔ˊmærəˌtaɪm〕 *adj.* 海上的；近海的
  interisland 〔ˌɪntəˊaɪlənd〕 *adj.* 島與島之間的
  dike 〔daɪk〕 *n.* 堤；溝   *let a person down* " 任其失敗 "
  banyan〔ˊbænjən; -jæn〕 *n.* 榕樹(＝ banian)

Cheng-kung) set up his military and civil administrations there in 1661 — after the Dutch occupiers surrendered to him, at the Dutch-built Fort Providentia, which was replaced in 1875 by Chihkan Tower. Tainan residents built a shrine to Koxinga in 1875, which can still be visited today. In addition there are 209 temples in Tainan, including the 32?-year-old Confucian Temple.

47. Are there any good beaches in Southern Taiwan?

Yes, there are a good number of them. The most famous — and perhaps the finest — among them is Kenting Beach, also the site of the now famous Caesar Park Hotel. Another beautiful beach is at Chuan Fan Hsih (Sail Rock), just south of Kenting. Both are romantic tropical beaches with just the right ingredient —white sand.

48. Is it true that the Philippines are visible from Oluanpi?

Yes, on a clear day a person standing at the southernmost tip of Taiwan — Oluanpi — can see part of the northernmost island of the Philippines. It is also visible from the Sea Viewing Tower, which rests atop the mountain that is Kenting Forest Recreation Park.

** occupier 〔'ɑkjə,paɪə〕 *n.* 占領者　　shrine〔ʃraɪn〕*n.* 廟
resident〔'rɛzədənt〕*n.* 居民　　tropical〔'trɑpɪkl̩〕*adj.* 熱帶的
ingredient〔ɪn'gridɪənt〕*n.* 成分
visible〔'vɪzəbl̩〕*adj.* 可見的

49. How big is Lanyu, where is it, and how does one get there?

Lanyu is a fairly small island with an area of only 45 square kilometers (17.37 square miles). It is situated 76 kilometers (47.5 miles) southeast of Taitung (Taitung is a city on Taiwan's southeastern coast.) Lanyu is reachable by both plane and ferry, from Taitung and Kaohsiung. The English name for Lanyu is Orchid Island.

50. Is Lanyu inhabited?

Yes, by the Yami — not the Ami — tribe of aborigines. They number only 2,600, and live in 6 compact villages on the coast. Each village is independent from the others, and each has private fishing areas and croplands. Villages have no chiefs, and fights — which are few — are settled by negotiation by the the people. Until very recently they ware still a stoneage tribe.

51. What is the Window on China?

It is a 30 hectare (74 acre) world in miniature that showcases famous or notable architectural structures of mainland China and Taiwan in a 1:25 scale. There are 68

** ferry〔'fɛrɪ〕n. 渡船　　aborigines〔,æbə'rɪdʒə,niz〕n. 原始的居民
compact〔kəm'pækt〕adj. 小巧的　　chief〔tʃif〕n. 酋長
settle〔'sɛtl〕v. 和解　　negotiation〔nɪ,goʃɪ'eʃən〕n. 談判
hectare〔'hɛktɛr〕n. 公頃　　miniature〔'mɪnɪətʃɚ〕n. 縮小之物
showcase〔'ʃo,kes〕v. 展示　　scale〔skel〕n. 比例

miniature structures, 48 of which replicate buildings or construction projects in Taiwan. The remaining 20 are miniatures of China mainland structures.

52. Please suggest a Central Taiwan tour.

Take three days. On the first day fly to Hualien and tour Taroko Gorge, proceeding on to lunch at Tienhsiang. Stay the first night at Lishan, the next morning proceeding on to Taichung to visit the Happy Buddha of Taichung, which is 26.8 meters (88 feet) tall, the tallest statue of its kind in Taiwan. Travel on to Sun Moon Lake, and stay there. Tour the lake in the morning and leave for Taipei overnight there.

53. Is there anything to see at Hsitou (Chitou)?

There are no tourist attractions, except for a 2,800-year-old tree that stands 46 meters (151 feet) tall. It is a place of serene beauty, noted for its verdant bamboo forests, tended and maintained as an experiment by the National Taiwan University. Hsitou is 2,488 hectares (6,148 acres) large, and is 80 kilometers (50 miles) south of Taichung.

** replicate〔ˊrɛplɪ͵ket〕*v.* 重複　　　Window on China　*n.* 小人國
proceed〔proˊsid〕*v.* 繼續進行　　overnight〔ˊovɚnaɪt〕*v.* 過夜
serene〔səˊrin〕*adj.* 寧靜的　　　verdant〔ˊvɝdnt〕*adj.* 青蔥的
tend〔tɛnd〕*v.* 照料

54. What is there special about the Grand Hotel?

Aside from being one of the most beautiful structures in Taiwan, it is said to have the largest lobby in the world: 45 meters long and 35 meters wide; its area is 16,953 square feet. Furthermore, the construction cost, when figured room by room, came to US$31,660 in 1973 dollars. Imagine renting a US$32,000 room for US$40 a night!

55. Where's the Queen's Head rock formation?

That is at Yehliu, or Wild Willow, on Taiwan's northern coast, less than one hour's drive from Taipei. Yehliu is famous for its coral rock formations, the Queen's Head perhaps the most famous among them. You can take a bus or a cab to get there, but a cab will cost you up to NT$2,000 for a round trip from Taipei.

** lobby〔'lɑbɪ〕*n*. 大廳   *come to* " 總數達… "
coral rock formations 珊瑚岩層

Group 3　History歷史

56. Who first established Taichung, and what has become of the city today?

The first group of settlers were from mainland China, some of whom established a village which they called Tatun. The Japanese, who occupied Taiwan for half a century, gave Tatun a new name, Taichung, which means "Central Taiwan." Present day Taichung is the third largest city in Taiwan and has a population exceeding 680,000.

57. How long were the Dutch on Taiwan?

From 1624 to 1661. They had considerable holdings, especially after they ousted the Spanish in 1642. They were in turn ousted in 1661 by the Ming Dynasty loyalist general, Cheng Cheng-kung (Koxinga).

58. What else has happened at Keelung?

A terrible earthquake hit the city on December 18, 1867. Then in August, 1884, during the 1884-5 Franco-Chinese war, French warships first bombarded and then occupied the city, and remained for eight months until the two governments agreed to a cease-fire. Then only ten years later,

---

** exceed〔ɪkˈsid〕*vt.* 超過

holding〔ˈholdɪŋ〕*n.*〔常用 *pl.*〕保有地；保有物

oust〔aʊst〕*vt.* 驅逐　　*in turn* "挨次"

bombard〔bɑmˈbɑrd〕*vt.* 砲轟

in 1895, Keelung became the first strategic location to be occupied by the Japanese, who then occupied Taiwan for 50 years.

59. Where is Tamsui, and what is its history?

Tamsui is on Taiwan's northwest coast; it is a small fishing port at the confluence of the Tamsui river and the Taiwan Strait. In 1629 the Spanish claimed it and built Fort San Domingo on a nearby hilltop. The Dutch then took control of Tamsui in 1642 after they had ousted the Spanish from Taiwan.

60. Is there anything else distinctive about Tamsui?

Yes. It is the site of Taiwan's oldest golf course, which the Japanese opened in 1919. Lu Liang-huan, or "Mr. Lu," who earned second place in the 1971 British Open, learned to play golf there as a caddy. Tamsui is also home to Tamkang University.

61. Who was Wu Feng?

He was a good friend of the aborigines of the Chiayi area, and is now one of Taiwan's heroes. As legend has it, in order to halt the aborigines' head-hunting practices, he tricked them into taking his head. When the aborigines discovered they had beheaded their friend, they immediately ceased these practices.

** strategic 〔strəˈtidʒɪk〕 *adj.* 戰略的
confluence 〔ˈkɑnfluəns〕 *n.* 滙流處　caddy 〔ˈkædɪ〕 *n.* 桿弟；拾球之小僮
halt 〔hɔlt〕 *v.* 停止　　behead 〔bɪˈhɛd〕 *v.* 斬首

62. What is the East Gate all about？The history behind it？

　　Once upon a time, a small part of present day downtown Taipei used to be a walled city. Reminders of that time are the city gates, notably the East Gate facing the Presidential Building from the center of a street junction several hundred yards away. The East Gate is one of four remaining gates of the five originally built. The massive walls themselves, with a total length of 5 Kilometers (3.1 miles), were torn down by the Japanese to make way for urban renewal.

63. Where was Santissima Trinidad？

　　That was the Spanish name for the port city now called Keelung. The Spanish occupied Keelung and adjoining stretches of coast from 1626 to 1642. They were an expeditionary force from the Philippines, and were driven out by the Dutch.

** *once upon a time* "從前"　　junction〔ˊdʒʌŋkʃən〕*n.* 會合處；交叉點
　　make way for "讓路給"　　urban〔ˊɝbən〕*adj.* 都市的
　　adjoining〔əˊdʒɔɪnɪŋ〕*adj.* 鄰接的
　　expeditionary〔ˌɛkspɪˊdɪʃənˌɛrɪ〕*adj.* 遠征的

Group 4 Culture 文化

64. What is Confucianism?

It is a code of values that, when executed, ensures so-
cial stability and harmonious relations through *jen*, or altru-
istic love. It is a philosophy rather than a religion, used
for two millenia by Chinese Imperial governments to main-
tain the status quo. It has more profoundly influenced the
Chinese and their culture than any other system of thought.

65. Where can I buy pieces of Chinese art?

At the Chinese Handicraft Mart at No. 1 Hsuchow Road
in Taipei. It's also known as the " one-stop shopping place "
for visitors to Taiwan because it offers such a large variety
of arts and crafts items. It is government-sponsored, so
prices are low and quality assured.

66. Who is the God of War I see in so many temples?

He is a war hero of the Romance of the Three King-
doms, a 14th Century popular novel. His name is Kuan
Kung, and he's also known as the God of Righteousness and
the Guardian of Business. There are 350 temples dedicated
to Kuan Kung, the most important of which is the Hsingtien
Temple in Taipei.

** altruistic〔͵æltru'ɪstɪk〕*adj.* 不自私的
  millenia〔mə'lɛnɪə〕*n.* 千年 (millenium 的複數型)
  status quo〔'stetəs'kwo〕*n.* 現狀　　mart〔mɑrt〕*n.* 市集
  righteousness〔'raɪtʃəsnɪs〕*n.* 公正　　guardian〔'gɑrdɪən〕*n.* 保護人

67. Describe Chinese jade.

Jade is derived from nephrite, also known as "soft jade." In its pure white form nephrite is known as white jade, but when it contains metallic particles, colors range from bluish-white to black result, and thus is called green jade, black jade, etc. Jadeite, mined in regions of Yunnan Province and Upper Burma, is harder, but is also white in its pure state. When impure, its colors range from rust to emerald green to lavender.

68. Why are there little animals on the ridges of Chinese-style roofs?

This tradition began in the 3rd Century B.C. when Prince Min of the State of Ch'i was strung up under a roof to die after he was defeated in battle. The people made effigies of the prince riding a hen, and put them on the roofs of their houses. Fierce dragons and gargoyles were added to keep the prince from escaping.

69. What are Taiwan's most important festivals?

Easily the three most important festivals are the Chinese Lunar New Year, the Dragon Boat Festival, and the Mid-autumn (Moon) Festival. Others of considerable importance are the Lantern Festival, Birthdays of Kuan Yin and Matzu, the Month of Ghosts, the Lovers' Festival and the Birthday of Cheng Huang.

**　be derived from** "由～獲得"　　nephrite〔'nɛfraɪt〕*n.* 軟玉
　jadeite〔'dʒedaɪt〕*n.* 硬玉　　impure〔ɪm'pjʊr〕*adj.* 不純的
　effigy〔'ɛfədʒɪ〕*n.* 雕像　　gargoyle〔'gɑrgɔɪl〕*n.* 怪人像

70. Do the Chinese have their own horoscope system?

Yes, our system is based on twelve-year cycles, each year represented by an animal. Each animal possesses characteristics and personalities which are unique to it, and people born in say, for instance, the Year of the Rat, would tend to possess the rat's characteristics.

71. Do people use this horoscope to tell fortunes?

Chinese fortune-telling is far more complex and detailed than the twelve-year cycle, but the average person may still use this system when considering a mate, though even this is getting rare.

** considerable〔kən'sɪdərəbl〕 *adj.* 值得注意的
  horoscope〔'hɔrə'skop〕*n.* 占星術　　mate〔met〕*n.* 配偶
  tell fortunes "算命"

Group 5 Taipei 台北

72. Are there many good restaurants in Taipei?

Yes, but they're far too numerous to list here. Let it suffice to say that most any kind of food from most everywhere on the globe can be had in Taipei, from fine Indian curry to delicate French croissants. Most important, though, is the abundance of restaurants representing all of the various Chinese cuisines, including those of Szechuan, Chekiang, Hunan, Shanghai, etc.

73. Please explain the history of Taipei.

Taipei is located in Northern Taiwan. It was proclaimed the provisional capital of the Republic of China on December 7, 1949, four years and six weeks after the island province had reverted to Chinese rule following a half century of Japanese colonial occupation (1895 — 1945). Because of its supreme importance to the Republic, Taipei was made a special municipality in July 1967, thus acquiring the same status as a province, and its mayor the same rank as a provincial governor.

74. Can you suggest an itinerary for a one-day tour or Taipei?

You should visit the Chung Cheng (Chiang Kai-shek Memorial Hall, the Presidential Square, Lungshan Temple, the Martyrs Shrine, the National Palace Museum and, if time permits, Hsimenting and Snake Alley.

** croissant〔krwɑ'sɑn〕 *n.* 新月形麵包　　revert〔rɪ'vɝt〕 *vi.* 復歸
provisional〔prə'vɪʒənl〕 *adj.* 臨時的　　itinerary〔aɪ'tɪnəˌrɛrɪ〕 *n.* 旅行路線

75. What can you tell me about the Chung Cheng Memorial Hall?

The Memorial Hall was designed in traditional Chinese architecture. The building itself covers 2 acres and is 245 feet high. It contains a 25-foot high bronze statue of Chiang Kai-shek, the late president, with the principal events of his life inscribed on the pedestal. Also, there are exhibition rooms and a theater on the ground floor.

76. Are there any other temples in Taipei besides the Lungshan Temple?

Yes, with over 5,000 temples and shrines dotting the island, there are sure to be quite a large number in Taipei alone. Notable among them is the Confucian Temple dedicated, of course, to the great sage Confucius (551 — 479 B.C.)

77. Which museums in Taipei are recommendable to a tourist?

The National Palace Museum is, of course, the most recommendable of all. In addition, the National Museum of History, the Taiwan Provincial Museum, and the Taipei Fine Arts Museum are also worth visiting.

** memorial〔məˊmorɪəl〕 *adj.* 紀念的；追悼的
inscribe〔ɪnˊskraɪb〕 *vt.* 銘刻
pedestal〔ˊpɛdɪstl̩〕 *n.* 半身塑像的座
dot〔dɑt〕 *vt.* 星散於 sage〔sedʒ〕 *n.* 聖人
recommendable〔͵rɛkəˊmɛndəbl̩〕 *adj.* 可推薦的
provincial〔prəˊvɪnʃəl〕 *adj.* 省的

78. Are there any parks in Taipei?

Several. One is the meticulously kept grounds area surrounding the Chiang Kai-shek Memorial Hall. With the National Theater, the Concert Hall and hundreds of meters of paths, it's a serenely beautiful site for an evening stroll. Nearby is the Taipei New Park, with a bandstand, pond and pagodas. Other noteworthy parks are the Sun Yat-sen Memorial Hall grounds, the Taipei Botanical Garden, and breathtaking Mt. Yangming National Park on the outskirts of Taipei.

79. What is the importance of the Sun Yat-Sen Memorial Hall?

This building is a tribute to the father of the Republic of China, Dr. Sun Yat-Sen. Dr. Sun Yat-sen was the man who overthrew the corrupt Ching Dynasty (1644 — 1911) and established the Republic of China in 1912. He is known worldwide for his formulation of the Three Principles of the People.

80. Is Taipei a good place to shop?

Taipei is teeming with shops, stalls and department stores, selling goods at relatively low prices. Districts such as Wanhua and Hsimenting attract billions of NT dollars worth of business per year, and are reknowned throughout the island as shoppers' paradises. One of the best features of shopping anywhere in Taiwan is the sopowners' willingness to bargain.

** meticulously〔mə'tɪkjələslɪ〕*adv*. 極端注意瑣事地
serenely〔sə'rinlɪ〕*adv*. 安詳地　　stroll〔strol〕*n*. 漫步
bandstand〔'bænd,stænd〕*n*. 音樂台　　pagoda〔pə'godə〕*n*. 寶塔
tribute〔'trɪbjut〕*n*. 表尊敬的行為　　*be teeming with* "富於"

附錄 導遊人員管理規則

第　一　條　本規則依發展觀光條例第四十七條規定訂定之。

第　二　條　導遊人員應經交通部觀光局或其委託之有關機關測驗及訓練合格，取得結業證書，並受旅行業僱用或受政府機關、團體爲舉辦國際性活動而接待國際觀光旅客之臨時招請，請領執業證後，始得執行導遊業務。

第　三　條　導遊人員分專任導遊及特約導遊。

　　　　　　專任導遊指長期受僱於旅行業執行導遊業務之人員。特約導遊指臨時受僱於旅行業或受政府機關、團體爲舉辦國際性活動而接待國際觀光旅客之臨時招請而執行導遊業務之人員。

　　　　　　前項專任導遊人員以受僱於一家旅行業爲限。

第　四　條　導遊人員應思想純正、品德良好、身心健全、儀表端正，並具有左列資格：

一、中華民國國民年滿二十歲，現在國內連續居住六個月以上並設有戶籍者。

二、經教育部認定之國內外大專以上學校畢業者。

第　五　條　有左列情事之一者，不得爲導遊人員：

一、曾犯內亂、外患罪者，經判決正確者。

二、非旅行業或非導遊人員非法經營旅行業或導遊業務，經查獲處罰未逾三年者。

三、導遊人員有違本規則，經撤銷導遊人員執業證未逾五年者。

第　六　條　導遊人員測驗科目如左：

　　　　　　一、筆試：

　　　　　　　　㈠ 三民主義。

　　　　　　　　㈡ 本國歷史、地理。

　　　　　　　　㈢ 導遊常識。

　　　　　　　　㈣ 外國語文。

　　　　　　二、口試。

第　七　條　參加導遊人員測驗合格者，應接受專業訓練，並依規定繳交訓練費用。

　　　　　　導遊人員訓練之課目，由交通部觀光局擬訂，報請交通部核定。

第　八　條　導遊人員應加入中華民國觀光導遊協會爲會員，並應參加交通部觀光局舉辦之在職訓練。

第　九　條　專任導遊人員執業證，應由旅行業填具申請書，檢附有關證件，向交通部觀光局請領：解僱時導遊人員應將其執業證，繳送旅行業轉送交通部觀光局。

第　十　條　特約導遊人員執業證，應由中華民國觀光導遊協會填具申請書附有關證件，向交通部觀光局請領，於特約導遊受僱用或臨時招請時發給使用，並按月報請交通部觀光局備查。

第 十 一 條　特約導遊人員受僱用或臨時招請時，應由中華民國觀光導遊協會發給臨時服務證，填明僱用或臨時招請單位、期間及導遊地區，連同導遊人員執業證交由特約導遊人員使用執業完畢後送繳中華民國觀光導遊協會保管。

第 十 二 條　政府機關、團體爲舉辦國際性活動而接待國際觀光旅客，臨時招請導遊人員時，應函請交通部觀光局轉送中華民國觀光導遊協會指派之。

第 十 三 條　導遊人員執業證應每年查驗一次，其有效期間爲三年，期滿應申請交通部觀光局換發。

第 十 四 條　導遊人員取得結業證書，連續三年未申請執業證執行導遊業務者，應重行參加導遊人員訓練結業，領取執業證，始得執行導遊業務。

第 十 五 條　導遊人員領得執業證，因故遺失或毀損，應具書面敍明原因，申請補發或換發。

第 十 六 條　導遊人員執業時，應接受僱用之旅行業或招請之機關、團體之指導與監督。

第 十 七 條　導遊人員應依僱用之旅行業或招請之機關、團體所安排之觀光旅遊行程執業，非因臨時特殊事故,不得擅自變更。

第 十 八 條　導遊人員執業時，應佩帶執業證，並攜帶旅行業或中華民國觀光導遊協會發給之服務證，以備查驗。

第 十 九 條　導遊人員執業時，如發生特殊或意外事件，除應即時作妥當處置外，並應將經過情形儘速向交通部觀光局報備。

第 二 十 條　交通部觀光局爲督導導遊人員，得隨時派員檢查其執業情形。

　　　　　　前項檢查必要時得會同有關機關執行之。

第二十一條　導遊人員有左列情事之一者，由交通部或交通部觀光局予以獎勵或表揚之。

一、爭取國家聲譽、敦睦國際友誼表現優異者。

二、宏揚中華文化、維護善良風俗有良好表現者。

三、維護國家安全、協助社會治安有具體表現者。

四、服務旅客週到、維護旅遊安全有具體事實表現者。

五、熱心公益、發揚團隊精神有具體表現者。

六、撰寫報告內容詳實、提供資料完整有參處價值者。

七、研究著述，對發展觀光事業或執行導遊業務具有創意可供採擇實行者。

八、連續執行導遊業務十五年以上，成績優良者。

九、其他特殊優良事蹟者。

第二十二條　導遊人員不得有左列行為：

一、執行導遊業務時，言行不當。

二、遇有旅客患病，未予妥為照料。

三、誘導旅客採購物品或為其他服務收受回扣。

四、向旅客額外需索。

五、向旅客兜售或收購物品。

六、以不正當手段收取旅客財物。

七、私自兌換外幣。

八、為旅客媒介色情或有妨害善良風俗之行為。

九、玷辱國家榮譽，損害國家利益。

十、不遵守專業訓練之規定。

十一、將執業證服務證借供他人使用。

十二、無正當理由延誤執業時間或擅自委訓他人代為執業。

十三、拒絕主管機關或警察機關之檢查。

十四、停止執行導遊業務期間擅自執業。

十五、擅自經營旅行業務或為非旅行業執行導遊業務。

第二十三條　導遊人員違反本規則規定者，由交通部觀光局依發展觀光條例第四十條之規定處罰，並報交通部備查。

第二十四條　本規則自發布日施行

全國最完整的文法書 ☆☆☆

文法寶典

▶ 劉 毅 編著

這是一套想學好英文的人必備的工具書,作者積多年豐富的教學經驗,針對大家所不了解和最容易犯錯的地方,編寫成一套完整的文法書。

本書編排方式與眾不同,首先給讀者整體的概念,再詳述文法中的細節部分,內容十分完整。文法說明以圖表爲中心,一目了然,並且務求深入淺出。無論您在考試中或其他書中所遇到的任何不了解的問題,或是您感到最煩惱的文法問題,查閱**文法寶典**均可迎刃而解。例如:哪些副詞可修飾名詞或代名詞?(P.228);什麼是介副詞?(P.543);那些名詞可以當副詞用?(P.100);倒裝句(P.629)、省略句(P.644)等特殊構句,爲什麼倒裝?爲什麼省略?原來的句子是什麼樣子?在**文法寶典**裏都有詳盡的說明。

例如,有人學了**觀念錯誤的**「假設現在式」的公式,

> If + 現在式動詞……,主詞 + shall(will, may, can)+ 原形動詞

只會造:If it rains, I will stay at home.

而不敢造:If you *are* right, I *am* wrong.

　　　　If I *said* that, I *was* mistaken.

　　　　(If 子句不一定用在假設法,也可表示條件子句的直說法。)

可見如果學文法不求徹底了解,反而成爲學習英文的絆腳石,對於這些易出錯的地方,我們都特別加以說明(詳見 P.356)。

文法寶典每冊均附有練習,只要讀完本書、做完練習,您必定信心十足,大幅提高對英文的興趣與實力。

◉ 全套五冊,售價**900**元。市面不售,請直接向本公司購買。

●台北市●
重南書局　文翔書局　衆文書局　永大書局　巨擘書局　新智書局　正文書局　弘雅書局　文友書局　博大書局　致遠書局　千華書局　曉園書局　建宏書局　宏業書局　文康書局　光統書局　文源書局　翰輝書局　文化書局　正元書局　天龍書局　金石堂　文化廣場　建德書報社　貞德書報社　百全書報社　聯宏書報社　聯豐書報社　華一書報社　偉正書報社　恒立書報社　中台書報社　建興書局　文笙書局　大中國書局　國聯書局　宏一書局　宏昇書局　百文書局　鴻儒堂書局　廣城書局　學語書局　南陽書局　三友書局　華星書局　新學友書局　來來百貨　永漢書局　力行書局　泰堂書局　金橋圖書股份有限公司　文普書局　力霸百貨　集太祥書局　偉群書局　萬泰書局　明志書局　宏玉書局　興來百貨　文佳書局　自力書局　誼美書局　水準書局　中美書局　頂淵書局　今日書局　長樂書局　德昌書局　敦煌書局　松芳書局　弘文書局　統領書局　啟文書局　永琦書局　鴻源百貨　敬恒書局　新光百貨　益群書局　聯一書局　朝陽堂　六福堂書局　博文堂書局　益民書局　捨而美書局　百葉書局　今博書局　鑫日書局　太華書局　平峰書局　百合書局　朝陽書局　天才學局　久大書　香世界　東利書局　聯合資訊　天下電腦　信宏書局　校園書局　中興大學圖書部　合歡書局　博聞堂書局　政大書局　再興書局　建安書局　文理書局　華一書局　伯樂書局　東光百貨公司　宏明書局　建國書局　中建書局　師大書局　浦公英書局　夢溪書局　時報出版社　宏欣書局　桂冠出版社　九章出版社　開發書局　智邦書局　永豐餘　永星書局　漢昇書局　慈暉書局　達仁書局　新興書局　明志工專　崇文圖書　廣奧書局　進文堂書局　福勝書局　台大書局　書林書局　景儷書局　香草山書局　漢記書局　光啟書局　增文堂書局　富美書局　益中書局　葉山書局　漢文書局　師大書苑　學海書局　克明書局　華城書局　崇暉書局　來來書局　青草地書局　實踐書坊　人人書局　文軒書局　升華書局　大學書局　東成書局　長青書局　玉山書局　亨得利書局　文達書局　光華書局　冠德書局　宗記書局　士林書局　宇文書局　檸檬黃書局　大漢書局　信加書局　勝一書局　兒童百科書局

●永和●
東豐書局　國中書局　宇城書局　潮流書局　文德書局　大方書局　超群書局　文山書局　三通書局

●中和●
景新書局　華陽書局

●新店●
華泰書局　文風書局　勝博書局　文山書局　宏德書局

●板橋●
永一書局　優豪電腦　建盈書局　賢明書局　流行站百貨　恒隆書局　啟文書局　峰國書局　文林書局　文人書局　文城書局　大漢書局　大有爲書局

●三重●
義記書局　日新書局　文海書局　百勝書局　仁人書局

●新莊●
珠海書局　鴻陽書局　文林書局　辰陽書局

崇文圖書

●泰山鄉●
大雅書局

●淡水●
文理書局　匯林書局　淡友書局　國寶書局　匯文書局　中外書局

●羅東●
翰林書局　統一書局　學人書局　三民學局　國泰書局　環華書局　國民書局

●宜蘭●
華山書局　金隆書局　新時代局　四季風書局　方向書局

●花蓮●
千歲書坊　中原書局　新生書局　精藝書坊

●台東●
徐氏書局　統一書局

●金門●
翰林書局　源成書局　金鴻福書局

●澎湖●
大衆書局　黎明書局

●桃園●
文化書局　中山書局　天寧書局　東方書局

東海書局
大新書局
奇奇書局
全國優良圖
書展藍源德
好學生書局
●中壢●
立德書局
文明書局
文化書局
貞德書局
建宏書局
博士書局
奇奇書局
大學書局
●新竹●
大學書局
昇大書局
六藝出版社
竹一書局
仁文書局
學府書局
文華書局
黎明書局
文國書局
金鼎獎書局
大新書局
文山書局
弘文書局
德興書局
學風書局
泰昌書局
滋朗書局
排行榜書局
光南書局
大華書報社
●苗栗●
益文書局
芙華書局
建國書局
文華書局
●基隆●
文粹書局
育德書局

自立書局
明德書局
中興書局
文隆書局
建國書局
文豐書局
●台中市●
宏明書局
曉園出版社
台中門市
滄海書局
大學圖書
供應社
逢甲書局
聯經出版社
中央書局
大眾書局
新大方書局
中華書局
文軒書局
柏林書局
亞勝補習班
文化書城
三民書局
台一書局
興大書局
興大書齋
興文書局
正文書局
新能書局
新學友學局
全文書局
國鼎書局
國寶書局
華文書局
建國書局
汗牛書屋
享聲唱片行
華中書局
逢甲大學
諾貝爾書局
中部書報社
中一書局
明道書局

振文書局
中台一專
盛文書局
●台中縣●
三民書局
建成書局
欣欣唱片行
大千書局
中一書局
明道書局
●彰化●
復文書局
東門書局
新新書局
台聯書局
時代書局
成功書局
世界書局
來來書局
翰林書局
一新書局
中山書局
文明書局
●雲林●
建中書局
大山書局
文芳書局
國光書局
良昌書局
三民書局
●嘉義市●
文豐書局
慶隆盛書局
羲豐書局
志成書局
大漢書局
書苑庭書局
學英公司
天才書局
學英書局
光南書局
嘉聯書報社
●嘉義縣●
建成書局

●台南縣●
全勝書局
博大書局
第一書局
南一書局
柳營書局
●台南市●
欣欣文化社
光南唱片行
嘉南書社
第一書局
東華書局
成功大學
書局部
成大書城
文山書局
孟子書局
大友書局
松文書局
盛文書局
台南書局
日勝書局
旭日書局
南台圖書
公　司
金寶書局
船塢書坊
南一書局
大統唱片行
國正書局
源文書局
永茂書報社
天才書局
●高雄縣●
延平書局
欣良書局
大岡山書城
時代書局
鳳山大書城
遠東大書城
天下書局
杏綱書局
統一書局
百科書局

志成書局
光遠書局
●高雄市●
高雄書報社
宏昇書局
理想書局
高文堂書局
松柏書局
三民書局
光南書局
國鼎書局
文英書局
黎明書局
光明書局
前程書局
尕行書局
登文書局
青山外語
補習班
六合書局
美新書局
朝代書局
意文書局
地下街
文化廣場
大立百貨公
司圖書部
大統百貨公
司圖書部
黎明文化
有前書局
建工書局
鐘樓書局
青年書局
瓊林書局
大學城書局
引想力書局
永大書局
杏莊書局
儒林書局
雄大書局
復文書局
致遠書局
明仁書局

宏亞書局
瀚文書局
天祥書局
廣文書局
楊氏書局
慈珊書局
盛文
光　統
圖書百貨
愛偉書局
●屏東●
復文書局
建利書局
百成書局
新星書局
百科書局
屏東書城
屏東唱片行
英格文教局
賢明書局
大古今書局
屏東農專
圖書部
順時書局
百順書局

Editorial Staff

- **編著**／林　凡
- **校訂**
  劉　毅・劉文欽・葉淑霞・卓美玲
  陳美月・鄭明俊・周美瑜・謝靜慧
- **校閱**
  John C. Didier・Bruce S. Stewart
  John H. Voelker・Kenyon T. Cotton
- **封面設計**／唐　旻
- **美編**／唐　旻・黃新家・林燕茹・謝淑敏
- **打字**／黃淑貞・倪秀梅・蘇淑玲・吳秋香
- **覆校**
  陳瑠琍・謝靜芳・蔡琇瑩・褚謙吉
  劉復苓・洪琴心

||||||||||||| ●學習出版公司門市部● |||||||||||||||

台北地區：台北市許昌街 10 號 2 樓 TEL：(02)2331-4060・2331-9209
台中地區：台中市綠川東街 32 號 8 樓 23 室
　　　　　TEL：(04)223-2838

|||||||||||||||||||||||||||||||||||||||||||||||

英語導遊考照速成（聽力口試篇）

編　　著／林　凡

發　行　所／學習出版有限公司　　　　　☎ (02) 2704-5525

郵 撥 帳 號／0512727-2 學習出版社帳戶

登　記　證／局版台業 *2179* 號

印　刷　所／裕強彩色印刷有限公司

台 北 門 市／台北市許昌街 10 號 2 F　　　☎ (02) 2331-4060・2331-9209

台 中 門 市／台中市綠川東街 32 號 8 F 23 室　☎ (04) 223-2838

台灣總經銷／紅螞蟻圖書有限公司　　　　☎ (02) 2799-9490・2657-0132

美國總經銷／Evergreen Book Store　　　☎ (818) 2813622

售價：新台幣一百五十元正

2000 年 12 月 1 日一版五刷

ISBN 957-519-074-2